THE END OF THE WORLD
AND BEYOND

The END *of the* WORLD *and* BEYOND

Continues

The Unexpected Life of

Oliver Cromwell Pitts:

Being an Absolutely Accurate

Autobiographical Account of My

Follies, Fortunes & Fate

Written by Himself

AVI

Algonquin Young Readers 2019

Published by
Algonquin Young Readers
an imprint of Algonquin Books of Chapel Hill
Post Office Box 2225
Chapel Hill, North Carolina 27515-2225

a division of
Workman Publishing
225 Varick Street
New York, New York 10014

Printed in the United States of America.
Published simultaneously in Canada by Thomas Allen & Son Limited.
Design by Carla Weise.

LIBRARY OF CONGRESS CATALOGING-IN-PUBLICATION DATA
Names: Avi, 1937– author.
Title: The end of the world and beyond : continues
The unexpected life of Oliver Cromwell Pitts: being an absolutely
accurate autobiographical account of my follies, fortunes & fate
written by himself / Avi.
Description: First edition. | Chapel Hill, North Carolina :
Algonquin Young Readers, 2019. | Sequel to: The unexpected life of
Oliver Cromwell Pitts. | Summary: After his thievery conviction in 1724,
Oliver Cromwell Pitts is sent from England across the Atlantic to America,
where he is enslaved on a tobacco farm, never giving up on finding his
sister, Charity, brought to the colonies on a different ship.
Identifiers: LCCN 2018014555 | ISBN 9781616205652
(hardcover : alk. paper)
Subjects: | CYAC: Prisoners—Fiction. | Indentured servants—Fiction. |
Slavery—Fiction. | United States—History—Colonial period,
ca. 1600–1775—Fiction. | LCGFT: Historical fiction.
Classification: LCC PZ7.A953 Eq 2019 | DDC [Fic]—dc23
LC record available at https://lccn.loc.gov/2018014555

10 9 8 7 6 5 4 3 2 1
First Edition

For my sister, Emily

THE END OF THE WORLD
AND BEYOND

The Year 1725

CHAPTER ONE

In Which I Experience a Terrible Mid-Atlantic Storm.

The *Owners Goodwill*—a two-masted ship—was in the middle of the Atlantic Ocean when it shuddered and heeled hard over as if attacked by a huge sea monster. It was, in fact, a powerful storm that had swept down upon us. Its abrupt and tremendous ferocity spun our vessel and us convict passengers all topsy-turvy. Since iron chains had been clamped round our necks and then bolted to the lower deck planking, this wild whirling of the ship caused us great pain, as if we were being hanged by iron rather than rope.

In the hurly-burly, the excrement buckets broke loose and our entire area, as well as we convicts, began to stink like the filthiest of muck-pits. To add to our woefulness, some of the overhead planking sprang apart so that we were drenched by numb-cold seawater. The darkness on our deck also meant we didn't know the hour.

You may be sure my fellow felons and I would have much preferred the freedom to stand on the main deck to confront the danger and our God. Terror (and misery) was further enlarged because the hatchway leading up had been fastened shut in fear that we prisoners might mutiny.

"Unchain us," someone shouted.

"Let us go free," called another.

"Don't let me perish," I cried.

Though the tumbling of the ship continued to increase even as our yells and screams of desperation grew louder, there was no response, much less rescue. Indeed, as the clamors of the tempest became ever more riotous, and the ship's movements still wilder, it appeared for a certainty that our ship would founder. To express our circumstance in blunter words: the *Owners Goodwill* was about to sink to the bottom of the sea with every one of us—including me—trapped within.

In awful anguish, my thoughts went to my home on the southern coast of England, where I was born and lived my contented youth. I thought of my beloved sister, Charity. I recalled those times I spent with my frustrating father, who liked to spurt worldly sayings. One of those expressions, "He who is born to be drowned will never be hanged," now filled my head. For the truth is, just prior to my voyage, I had been sentenced to be hanged for thievery from the Tyburn gallows in London, England. Though I am pleased to inform you that I avoided that dread unfortunacy, it seemed as if there, in the middle of the Atlantic, I was destined to drown.

How did I—a boy of twelve years of age—ever come to be in such a desperate situation?

CHAPTER TWO

Which Reveals How I, a Freeborn English Boy, Was Exiled from My Home, Put in Chains, and Placed Aboard a Convict Ship.

No one knows his or her life better than the person who has lived it. Yet, having previously related the true events of my young life in the first volume of this autobiography,* I have been called "bedlam-brained." Some have gone so far as to claim I invented it all, as if I were some scribbling book-breeder so desperate for money I tumbled into fiction. Yet, by my faith, be assured that all of what I set down on these pages—my books of

---

* *The Unexpected Life of Oliver Cromwell Pitts: Being an Absolutely Accurate Autobiographical Account of My Follies, Fortunes & Fate*

misadventure, if you will—is as heart-whole as I can recall it. Yes, it was all unexpected, but I have written it down as I truly lived it.

To remind you of my situation:

As an ordinary boy of twelve years, living in the small town of Melcombe Regis in southwest England where I had been born, I woke on November 12, 1724, to find my family home all but destroyed by a fierce, fast-moving storm. To add to this catastrophe, my father had vanished, I knew not where. As for my sister, Charity, she was in London. (My mother, alas, died when I was born, so I have no memory of her at all.)

Being deserted, and desperate to feed myself, I took some twenty-three shillings from what I truly believed was an abandoned shipwreck—which it was not. Nonetheless I was put into the children's poorhouse where I was much abused. But I escaped and headed for London in search of my older and beloved sister, Charity, that she might—as she always had done—take care of me.

I had barely fled Melcombe Regis when I was caught by a Mr. Sandys, a lawless, fierce rogue, who in turn eased me into the hands of the masked highwayman Captain Hawkes. Hawkes, an underling of England's most notorious criminal, Jonathan Wild, enrolled me as one of his shoulder shams, which is to say, a thief.

In London, I found my sister, but, to my great distress,

she had become a common pickpocket. We escaped Mr. Wild and the law, searched and found our unsatisfactory father, in hopes he would solve our momentous difficulties. Instead, the three of us were arrested and brought to trial at the Old Bailey Courthouse. At that time we were all found guilty and sentenced to hang upon the gallows.

We surely would have danced at the end of that dismal rope if Father—a lawyer, whose knowledge of law was deep—had not bribed his Lordship, the honorable judge. That bribe freed my father and changed my punishment and Charity's: Instead of being hanged, she and I were to be transported to the American plantations thousands of miles from home where we would be enslaved for seven long years. Our sole comfort was that we would remain together.

On the day we were to board the oceangoing ships, Charity and I were bound together, and midst a great parade of prisoners, were marched through London streets. Though we were to become slaves for the duration of our sentences, Londoners exhibited their famous sense of humor by calling us convicts "His Majesty's seven-year passengers."

None of us felons enjoyed the jest.

Being linked by iron, and love, Charity and I walked hand in hand. Insofar as Father came freely by our side, I asked him where he would go.

To my surprise he said, "Once I have raised enough funds I intend to go to America and join you so we can be reunited."

We were led down to the Thames River embankment. At the last moment, Charity and I were parted and put on separate ships, presumably bound to different ports in America. Desperate, I reached for her, but all I could hold on to was a bit of lace from her sleeve cuff. My last cry to her was, "I will find you, Charity! I promise!" And I waved that bit of lace like a tiny flag.

I do not think anyone saw it.

CHAPTER THREE

Contains a Tiny Chapter about an Enormous Subject.

It was my sister, Charity, some six years older than me, who, in the absence of my mother, had raised me by hand. Truly, Charity was the light that illuminated my young life and in return I loved her beyond any other mortal. Ever patient, ever loving, she taught me to be cheerful, optimistic, and kindly, come what may. People may mock what they choose to call these gentle virtues, but I have endeavored to live my life with these qualities.

Thus, when my sister and I were separated, she to one unknown destination, I to another, it was the most unbearable moment of my life. That bit of lace was all I had of her. Oh, how I clung to it. Oh, how I wept over it.

It should come as no surprise, therefore, that my desire, my longing to find Charity, became the primary motivation of my new life. That incentive, that need, may be considered a footnote to every sentence, page, and action in this book.

As to whether I achieved my goal of reuniting with my beloved sister, you shall have to read my book to find out.

CHAPTER FOUR

In Which I Board a Convict Ship.

In London, despite a torrent of tears over my separation from my sister, I was obliged to board the *Owners Goodwill*—a name, I assure you, I did not invent. A brig of some eighty tons, the ship had two masts, was square-sterned, deep-waisted, and steered by wheel. Her captain was Elijah Krets, a spite-tempered, hufty-tufty man, well suited for the ship's previous satanic service, that of a chattel slave ship. Now he and the *Owners Goodwill* were in the lucrative if lamentable business of transporting British convicts to North America. His principal cargo was ninety felons, one of which was me.

When I came upon the vessel, I was registered as being safe ("safe" surely being the most ironical of words) on board. That allowed the ship's business investors to be paid five pounds by the Crown treasury to transport me to the new world.

My father had managed to slip a few shillings into my pocket just before I was taken from the English shore. Nevertheless, the *Owners Goodwill*'s first mate, a bulbous bully by the name of Mr. Babington, searched all of us convicts—a thief stealing from thieves—and relieved me (among others) of my cash. "You'll have no need to purchase anything," he told me. "We shall fill all your needs."

I was so distraught by my leave-taking from Charity that it came into my head to free myself by leaping off the boat. No sooner did I have that thought than one of the other convicts did what I was considering. That is, having sufficiently starved in prison, his thin wrists allowed him to slip his chains and attempt a leap to liberty. But before he could achieve his vaulting ambition, he was blocked, and his ill-considered craving for freedom was brutally beaten out of him by Mr. Babington.

After observing this valuable lesson in shipside custom, the rest of us convicts—including me—were easily forced to the tween deck. This was the level between the open main deck and the even deeper cargo space—the hold. The ceiling over our heads was no more than four and a half feet high, the deck twenty-eight feet wide and fifty-five feet long. It was as if we were being fitted into a group coffin.

Because I was a boy, and somewhat small for my age, the low-slung ceiling of the deck was of no particular hindrance to me—assuming I could stand. But it was agonizing to those who were adults. Their souls were already stooped; now their bodies were too.

My chains were linked to six adult convicts, a group called a "mess." Our padlocked iron shackles were also affixed to the deck planks, so that our movements were much restricted.

How did I ever come to this? I asked myself ten million times as I clutched that bit of Charity's lace and used it to wipe away my tears. Where was my beloved sister being sent? All well to promise to find her, but how? And where? Would we be near each other, or far apart? Needless to say, I had no answers to these despairing questions. That said, I do believe my disquiet about her allowed me to think less of myself and thereby reduced my pain.

Meanwhile, Captain Krets issued his commands: His crew merrily sang up the *Owners Goodwill*'s anchor, unfurled her sails, and caught a breeze. The ship dropped down the Thames River, paused at Plymouth, found a southwesterly wind, and cruised out upon the open, swelling sea, and headed for America, which in my mind was but another word for the unknown.

Once I was on the ship, I had no idea where I was going or what would happen to me when and if I reached my unnamed destination. My journey's end could have been cold Newfoundland, or the hot West Indies, or anywhere in between. Upon reaching the colonies I would be sold to a local free citizen who would become my absolute master for at least seven years. What labor he might command me to do, I had no idea.

The law said that if I returned to England before my time was out, I would, without further ado, be hanged. My only remedy was to be fully pardoned by a judge and I was quite sure no judge sailed with us.

Further, it was shared knowledge among my fellow prisoners that one of ten convicts died on the voyage to America. My messmates informed me that just as many would perish of illness soon after landing in the colonies. The climate was that cruel. "Seasoning" was the gentle term for avoiding an early death.

In other words, my life was at great hazard. If, at that moment—to return to an earlier metaphor—I thought of my future as a book and chanced to open these pages so as to skip to the ending—as some impatient readers do—I would have been unable to find so much as one word of comfort printed therein. I was required to turn the painful pages of my life one by one so as to experience my forbidding fate.

I humbly beg you to do the same.

CHAPTER FIVE

In Which, for Those Desirous of Embarking on an Ocean Cruise, I Provide a Brief Description of Its Many Delights.

Nothing assures us of the rightfulness of the world as our own good fortune. By equal measure, I have come to learn that those who do not suffer, judge those who do suffer do so because of their own faults. Therefore—so the belief goes—those who have been punished by life (or the English law, which is harsher) are deserving of their punishment. Indeed, the common policy is that more suffering will cure such persons of their misery. It would be as if you went to a surgeon with a broken leg, and he decided the best cure would be to break your other leg. Such is the enlightened way of the modern world.

What then were the conditions that we felons enjoyed during the voyage of the *Owners Goodwill*?

Item: There was no saying how long the voyage would take, seven weeks or seven months. The time lay with the whim of the winds and the captain's nautical skills. Of course, some ships simply sank.

Item: As I mentioned, because there were no windows on our lower deck, it was difficult to say what time of day or night it was. At best, my close confinement was dim during days and darkful at night. Indeed, day and night seemed to merge. Time became an unending fog. But then, as the saying goes, an idle man needs no clock.

Item: Without portholes on our deck, there was no ventilation, so that the air we breathed was never fresh but always foul, the stench altogether turpie.

Item: Each day at noon (I believe) I was fed a scant pound of bad bread—oft weighted with wiggly worms—plus oversalted and putrid meat. Daily drink—if I got it—consisted of a slight pint of foul water.

Item: We slept upon the bare deck planks.

Item: Some of us were dressed in shirts and trousers of canvas. Some, like me, had shoes. Many wore naught but shreds and went barefoot. Regardless, in a short time, all clothing (including mine) was reduced to rags, tatters being the universal fashion of the poor.

Item: There were more lice than men. During the voyage countless days were filled by catching and crushing them. Many an hour passed with the only sound being *click, click, click.*

Item: Buckets of feces and urine were always open, and since we were chained, few of us could use those pails and perforce, did without.

Item: None of us were clean. Many had open, rotten-ish sores, which offered their own offensive stench. Some had wounds that festered with pale yellow maggots, which had more life than their hosts.

Item: A fair number of my fellow convicts, having spent months in abysmal London prisons, were famished when they boarded. Several were ill with diseases I am unable to name. I do know that on the *Owners Goodwill* seasickness became the norm. Jail-fever, better known as typhus, was also common. What's more, during our voyage, those who had been ill generally became worse. I cannot say what caused me to stay healthy. Perhaps it was because I was in the London prison for such a short time, and Father purchased my food.

Item: No physician was on the ship.

Item: In the first two weeks of our voyage, a few felons perished. That was the fate of both a frail lad of six and an eighty-year-old man, the bookends, if you will, of our company. Their corpses were stuffed into sacks, weighted with ballast stones, and dropped into the sea without benefit of clergy or kindness. We all assumed others would die before we reached America and could only pray that we would be spared.

In short, the only thing that distinguished our situation from Hell was that with us, it was always cold.

Was anyone happy to be leaving England? During our first night on the ship—once we were all chained down, the hatches bolted tight and daylight banished—our deck was filled with weeping, praying, and lengthy lamentations, punctuated now and again by halting hymns sung woefully off-key, more like the howls of dogs than a musical chorus of pious men.

I beg your forgiveness for providing all these gross details, but truth is often held up as a shining ideal. Most people, when they ask for truth, think of it as something good. You may trust me when I remind you that truth can also be horrific.

My father had a motto: "People care nothing for suffering. To get on you must mask your heart with false smiles." On the *Owners Goodwill*, this belief—as you shall see—was put to an extreme test.

CHAPTER SIX

In Which I Reveal My Life as a Convict.

My fellow shipboard convicts were all males. When we departed from England, the youngest was that boy of six, who had tried to steal a small saucer from a Covent Garden coffee shop. He had been knocked down (and heroically captured and arrested) by a courageous young aristocrat with a long, sharp sword.

Our eldest felon was the stooped and grizzled man of eighty years who attempted to make away with a woman's penny-purse along the Strand in London. When a hue and cry was sounded, a righteous (and riotous) mob tripped the fellow up by his antique heels. No matter that the penny-purse the old man stole proved empty. The jury—after a meticulous trial of five minutes—found him profoundly guilty and the wise judges, determining what was right and fitting, sentenced him to a full seven years of hard labor in America.

As I already informed you, both boy and old man died during the first weeks of our voyage. I prayed they moved out of our floating hell to a fair heaven. Hardly a wonder that many a time I often wept, fearful I would die.

It was hard to know which shocked me more, the crimes (big and small) of my fellow convicts or the legal system that branded them as felons. What was even more appalling: I was considered one of them.

How came this policy of punishment by transportation? The government theory was, it decreased Great Britain's criminal population, gave felons a humane chance of life, provided needful labor to the colonies, and was cheaper than maintaining prisons in England.

I leave it to your own intelligence to decide which the foremost reason was.

How did felons feel? Transportation was considered such a dreadful existence that some begged to be hanged.

How did I feel? The change in my life from my time in Melcombe Regis had happened so quickly—a matter of weeks—that I was bewildered, frightened, and considered myself abandoned. While I could understand the word—"felon"—whereby I had been labeled, there seemed to be no reason for it. It was as if my body was in one world, even as my thoughts remained in another. I hardly knew myself.

But perhaps because I was so young, small for my age, had a winsome smile, and was a friend to all, the men of my mess liked to talk to me, to impart what they thought was knowledge. What I learned mostly was that when my elders gave me advice, the guidance they offered was nothing they themselves had followed. It was that old adage: "What you might have done might have made you mighty."

In my own mess of fellow convicts, the crimes we had committed were varied. Three had been forced off their farms and walked to London in hopes of continued existence. Unable to find employment, they were arrested when they sought unlawful ways to keep themselves from starving to death.

One man in my mess had been a masked highway robber, the wearing of a mask in itself being a hanging offence, never mind the wealth he stole. Another had filched an infant's cushion—measuring six inches by six inches—from a sedan chair.

Hardly a wonder that the English laws to protect property were called "the bloody codes."

No matter the crime, we felons were all treated with brutal equality. Food was thrown at us. Questions refused. Hurts or illnesses ignored.

One exception: Our captain—Mr. Krets—took particular pleasure in abusing one of my messmates who had the legal name of John Trevis. For reasons I never learned, Mr. Trevis preferred to be called Moco Jack.

(Perhaps to disguise themselves, felons often took different names. One William Hudson was known as "Thickhead," without his head being unusual in any way that I could observe.)

Moco Jack was a small, skinny man—dry boned as people might say—a spiderish sort of fellow, all elbows and knees, shanks and arms. He had intense black eyes, was as bald as a stone, and had a reddish scar across his forehead, which enhanced his palpable fierceness. Forever sullen, he never, that I saw, so much as smiled. To look upon him and hear his talk was to grasp that he was one third anger, another third resentment, and the final third a deep reservoir for revenge.

That Moco Jack and I were chained together was pure chance. It meant however that I told him about my wrongdoings. He told me about his.

"My crime?" he informed me. "When I didn't move fast enough from a London constable's path, he called me a base brute. I struck him and that one blow is costing me seven years of my life. But I promise you, I shall live to return to London, seek him out, and suck him dry of blood."

Moco Jack was forever urging us felons to rise up and mutiny, to take command of the ship and liberate ourselves. All of us cherished the idea, but none had the will to run the hazard. Speaking for myself, I was too fearful of failing and having my punishment increased by more years of hard labor. I suspect others felt the same.

Another felon's story had greater impact on my life.

Rufus Caulwell was a man in his forties who, in London, had been apprehended for stealing a ten-ounce bag of barley with which he intended to feed his famished children and wife. He had not learned civilization's code of decency: that it is far better to let your children and wife waste away with hunger than steal a halfpenny's worth of food. For Mr. Caulwell's vile transgression against the social order, he had been sentenced to seven years' transportation.

"I don't intend to stay in America long," he confided one day in a rough whisper.

"How so?"

"In Newgate prison I met a man who knew a man who said he had a way to get back to England from America."

"And what is that?" I said, eager for ideas.

"A swamp."

"A *swamp*? What's a . . . swamp?" I asked, never having heard the word.

"A kind of American forest where the land isn't land, but water."

"Do such places truly exist?"

"Absolutely," he assured me.

"And where might you find this . . . swamp?"

"In America."

"Isn't America a vast place?"

"Never mind. I'll find it."

"And when you do, what then?"

"I shall discover my way."

"I wish you well," I said.

While I found it impossible to believe this story, I tucked it into a corner of my memory, keeping *swamp* as some kind of fairy-tale place. In this fashion, I learned that when prisoners are confined to small spaces, their minds travel to large worlds of their own invention.

In sum, on the *Owners Goodwill* there was death behind me, death in front of me, and death all around me. The only hope was a *swamp*, but I did not believe such a place truly existed.

And then, midst all this wretchedness, far worse arrived when—in the middle of the Atlantic Ocean—we were hit by that dreadful storm.

CHAPTER SEVEN

The Affrightful Storm.

As the storm roared and tumbled the ship into complete disorder, down on the tween deck, our pleas and entreaties for release continued unabated, along with banging on the overhead hatch by those who managed to reach it.

"Let us out."

"Open the door."

"Unchain us."

After what seemed an eternity, the way to our deck was opened and the first mate, Mr. Babington, appeared along with the cascading sea. In one hand, he held a small lit candle lantern. In his other hand was a key. The way he staggered about upon the rolling deck suggested he was jagged with drink.

The convicts threw questions at him:

"What is happening?"

"Are we about to sink?"

He provided no answers—save his frightened face—but stumbled around, mess by mess, and sprang our locks. The moment each group was released they raced for the companionway and clamored up.

At last my group was freed, and despite the wild heaving of the ship, I managed to reach the steps, and mounted as fast as I could until I came out upon the open main deck. It was so appalling that my immediate thought was that it would have been far better—and safer—if I had remained below.

The sea itself was a boiling cauldron of huge, froth-edged waves, which came crashing down upon the ship like heavy hammers and then swept across the deck with fearsome power. Just as I reached the top deck one of those colossal waves struck, then receded so quickly it sucked one of my brother felons into the sea, never to be seen again in this mortal world. His glugging screams of terror haunted me for many a day. Needless to say, our rescue jolly-boat was gone, though in that raging sea, it would have been useless.

Fierce rain attacked from the starboard side, piercing us like icy needles while the freezing wind howled the collective roars of a hundred wild beasts. So intense was the force of winds that to breathe I had to turn and cover my mouth and nose with a curled hand. Being small and light, I was obliged to cling to something—anything—to remain on the ship.

As for our sails, they had already been torn into tiny threads while the ropes and rigging were little more than lashing whips.

Woven into the shrieking winds came desperate cries of people pleading for God Himself to provide protection.

As for what I felt, aghast is too small a word. Try terrified. Though only twelve years of age, I was forced to consider: What would it be like to drown?

The constant wash of the sea over the *Owners Goodwill* was such that it was hard for me to distinguish if we were on the sea or already beneath it. It was as if the great waters that cover most of the earth resented our tiny claim of safety and sought to dissolve us into her lower depths.

To give my condition a truer sense, we were in the midst of "chaos," a Greek word that means the unformed matter of the world before God gave it shape, or so my father had taught me. At that hour, I felt as if the earth had reverted to that soulless state. Our safe ship seemed little more than a tiny thimble adrift upon the vastness of the salted sea.

No surprise then that my life appeared likely to be over. Yet, mark me, I treasured being alive. I therefore grasped ropes, rails, shrouds, shreds of sails, or my equally unfortunate shipmates, be they fellow convicts or sailors.

Then, as if from far away, I heard the voice of the captain cry: "Man the pumps. Man the pumps."

That call meant we were taking on water at a disquieting rate, either by rain, seawater falling down through hatches, or water leaking in via cracks upon the hull itself. No doubt the wild movements of the whirligig that our ship had become had sprung the planking, popping out the oakum used to seal the ship like so many lemon pips. We were becoming a sieve and liable to sink at any moment.

As for those pumps, they were crude machines used to empty the ship's hold of excess bilge water, or in this situation, the sea itself. These pumps were in the very bottom of the vessel, the most dangerous place to be. If the ship began to go down, there would be no way to get out. Yet there was no means of keeping the *Owners Goodwill* from sinking other than working these pumps. Am I clear? To avoid the greatest danger, some of us needed to go where the danger was even greater.

It was Mr. Babington, the first mate (no doubt shoved into sobriety by fulsome fright), who assembled the pump crew. Or rather, he snatched such men—sailors or felons— as he could and ordered them below. One of the persons he grabbed was me.

Please note: We convicts, on our way to enslavement, were being asked to save our own lives so we could live to be enslaved. Yet let it also be said, no one, least of all me, hesitated. Better to do than dilly-dally. In times of menace no moment is more precious than now. The past, in such a crisis, is irrelevant. And nothing seems more distant than the future. Therefore, I was willingly pushed down the steps, one of perhaps a dozen soggy souls. It felt wonderful to get away from the cutting winds and rain.

Deeper and deeper into the mungy hold we went, our way lit by two swaying lamps, their frail flames fluttering like feeble butterflies. As we made our way down the sheer steps it was necessary to cling to whatever would give stability, be it ropes, the man before (or behind) me, or the risers themselves.

When we reached the lowermost hold, it was to witness yet another pitiless place; it was as if we had descended into the belly of a monster, its food undigested. Not only was the air dungy and cold, stinking beyond all measure, we found an ocean of water swilling about in frothy, filthy waves. When I stepped into its coldness I sank to my chest and my teeth began to clatter like Spanish castanets.

The cargo—boxes, bales, and barrels—had, for the most part, broken free and was being thrown about in utter riot. I had come from a place where I might have been drowned to somewhere I could just as easily be crushed. The terror I felt on deck was in no way reduced.

Could anything live in such a place? Well, yes. I saw rats aplenty, some already drowned, others clinging to what they could. Indeed, rats and people were not so different save in size. But then the true equalizer of all God's creatures is fear. I was altogether sure I had come to the place where I must die among rats.

CHAPTER EIGHT

In the Bottommost Part of the Ship.

O ur first difficulty was to find the pumps. If we did find them, there was nothing to say that they—on this shameful ship—were in working order.

I had no idea who located them, but Heaven be praised they were located and discovered to be intact. These two pumps consisted of a pair of wooden cylinders into which rods had been placed. These rods had leather disks the circumference of those cylinders. When moved up and down by handles, the rods (with the leather disks) drew up the water and forced it through leather pipes and out of the ship.

Four of us set directly to work, two at either end of the pump's handles. Mind, while some of us worked the pumps, others stood about and shielded us from the cargo flying about.

33

As I pumped furiously and mindlessly, my eyes fell on a spot on the inside planking of the hull, where I perceived water dripping through. While we were pumping water out, water was leaking in. Impossible to say which had the greater volume or the faster flowing.

I shouted out what I had discovered, and one of the men splashed over to it and pressed his hands against the spot, attempting to hold back the sea. Another struggled back up the steps, presumably to tell the captain where we were leaking. He soon returned and shouted, "They're attempting to lay canvas against the hull."

When those who worked the pumps became exhausted—as I soon did—others took their places, so that the pumping never—not for a moment—ceased.

The work went on, up down, up down, for hours, four of us laboring all the time. Wallowing in the cold bilge, we were numb and mute. As we struggled, our little lamps cast dancing shadows high against the rib-like beams of the hull. These shadows appeared like the true image of our sinful souls, being the color of pitch and far larger than our own physical selves. When younger, I had attended a sermon in which it had been preached that men feared shadows because they revealed the inner soul. I recalled that notion then.

At one point, I felt a pricking on my shirt: A giant brown rat was climbing upon my back in search of safety.

I screamed and one of my mates snatched the rodent off and with a quick twist broke the creature's neck and flung its carcass somewhere in the hold; this, while the ship was tossing and turning, and the cargo still being hurled about in random.

From time to time I tried to gauge the level of the water in the hold, to see if I could determine if it was rising or falling; that is, were we sinking? I could not tell. Then, at some point, one of the pumps' leather tubes sprang a leak. We pumped harder.

All during this time, the roaring of the storm was a constant in my ears. But while the splashing of the water within the hull was unceasing, what I was listening for—though afraid to admit—was the fateful call from the captain: "Abandon ship!"

Instead one of the pumps broke.

CHAPTER NINE

In Which Something Startling Happens.

With one pump gone, our sole remedy was to work the remaining pump harder and faster. This meant that if the speed and force of our labors caused the first pump to break, we were now putting the second pump—and the ship—at even greater peril. But struggle we did, though to work in a frenzy without ceasing is a mindless experience. I was nothing but body: muscles, rhythm, and endless toil.

After what must have been hours—I lost all sense of time—as I continued to pump, I began to notice that the ship was no longer in a state of wild agitation.

"The storm must be abating," someone said.

No words could have been sweeter to my ears, heart, and arms.

"God be praised," was the general cry. "Hallelujah."

At length we felt a normal motion of ship and sea. Yet the hold of the *Owners Goodwill* was still full of water, so we continued pumping. Only after much more time passed did we see the water level going down. In contrast, my mind began to rise up into function again. At length, an order was shouted that we could come up from the hold.

Exhausted beyond all measure, but animated by a sense of reclaimed life, I pulled myself onto the deck to blink with astonishment at clear, bright, and true blue skies. The storm had utterly blown away. The sun was shining. The sea was calm. We were no longer in jeopardy of sinking. One often talks of an unpredictable person. But no one is more unpredictable than the sea or its storms. Happiness indeed to be alive. Surely, God had touched me with His hand of mercy. Trivial, perhaps, to say, but no less true; no moment is sweeter than the moment just after you thought you would have no more moments.

I was whole, but the ship itself had been reduced to floating wreckage. What had not been washed away— yards, rails, rope, jolly-boat, and sails—lay in tangled, knotted heaps. Fortunately, our two masts were still erect. Replacement sails and rope were in storage.

Alas, we also needed to consider our human losses.

Among the crew three had been swept away to a dismal drowning. As for us convicts, the number gone overboard was five.

There was no time to mourn. Despite our weariness, all crew and prisoners were set to work to put the *Owners Goodwill* to rights, to create order from disarray. With true goodwill, we worked side by side.

Only when much had been restored to decent order did something remarkable transpire.

I cannot say how, but crew and convicts had separated, and now stood apart in two distinct groups. We felons were in the waist of the ship, while the crew and captain were on the poop deck of the after-superstructure. Moreover, the captain and the first mate were now armed with cocked pistols, which they held in their hands in such fashion that we convicts could have little doubt they would use them on us.

"All right then," proclaimed Captain Krets, "felons will return to the lower deck to be rechained."

Please understand: From the beginning of the storm, the two groups—crew and convicts—had been working together, laboring under terrible conditions to save our lives. There was no us, no them. No free and unfree. We worked as one. All human.

Now we felons were being ordered to resume our servile station, to reinstate the order that was. After what we all had gone through together in the storm, the captain was reestablishing his authority and our status as convicts.

What happened next was not a simple thing.

Recall my messmate Moco Jack. Whereas the captain was a big man, Moco Jack was much smaller. But as I have indicated, there was much that was menacing about Moco Jack—his very red-rimmed eyes seemed to be discordful, as if to threaten. However, the captain had his position with which to dominate Moco Jack and used it often. Twice he had called out Moco Jack for some slight, and tied him to the foremast and flogged him with a cat-o'-nine-tails till he was bloody. Nothing new here: authority is the whip that subdues mankind.

Though the captain had lashed Moco Jack more than once for talking back to him, for being "saucy," and deprived him of his food when he complained about such treatment, Moco Jack remained—as demonstrated by the captain's actions—a threat. Nonetheless, he refused to bow down to the captain.

Moco Jack now stood before us felons, reduced (by storm and sickness) to some seventy or so in number. He was confronted by the captain and his crew, no more than fifteen. Of course, they were armed and we all were in a state of exhaustion, having come so close to perishing. Nonetheless, we stood there—these two groups—a challenge to one another. Life in miniature.

I felt a tremor of excitement to think that we could set ourselves at liberty. Still, I was aware that some of us might be shot dead in the attempt. I also experienced deep bone weariness. The truth is, what I wanted most of all was to rest and sleep in some safe, unmolested spot.

This then is how we stood: the two groups, one (small) but in the position of power, the other (large) and powerless, challenging one another with an unspoken knowledge that in a trice, our positions could be reversed. We would become masters. The captain and crew would become chained prisoners. The world turned upside down.

I could read as much on Moco Jack's face, his visible anger, and how his neck muscles quivered with tension; hands folded into fists, eyes fixed with palpable hatred upon Captain Krets. All of us felons looked at Moco Jack as our leader. It was an absolute certainty that we would follow him if he had moved so much as an inch toward mutiny.

He did move—by merely half an inch. That was enough for the captain to bring up his pistol and aim it right at my companion.

Consider this as well: It was common knowledge that flintlock pistols misfired half the time. Thus, Captain Krets's gun might fail, or it could just as well prove lethal.

Thus life and liberty hung in balance.

What happened next was this:

After a long moment, Moco Jack uncurled his fists and looked down with a submissive cast. I was unable to tell if he was playacting or being prudent, saving himself for another time. To my further astonishment, he turned and moved to the hatchway steps, and began to descend. From a leader of mutiny, he became the leader of our surrender. Not one word was exchanged.

What's more, we convicts followed in submissive silence.

Back we went to the lower deck. There we reassembled ourselves into our messes. Without resistance we sat and were rechained as before the storm.

I too submitted.

Why did this happen, without words or any overt action other than abject, silent surrender?

The best way I could understand it was this: My fellow felons had spent their entire lives trained to obey authority and authority's commands, so much so that they could not overleap that barrier, surely not in our state of fatigue. It suggested that much of the injustice of the world is caused by habit: the habits of the powerful, and the habits of the powerless.

This made a profound impression on me. Though at that time I did follow along, I made myself a vow that I would never again kneel to power. Had not my father taught me to reject authority? Was not my namesake—Oliver

Cromwell—the man who tumbled a king? Therefore, I would teach myself to resist authority in all ways—no matter how small—so that even as I was put back into chains, I rededicated myself to securing my liberty.

As I sat there bound to my messmates and the floor, I glanced at Moco Jack. It was as if he knew his moment had come and passed. I could see: it was not so much his courage that had failed him as his belief in himself.

He spoke to no one, with one exception, for the remainder of the voyage. What's more, he refused to look at anyone. To my greater mazement, as I looked at him, just after the events I have described, I saw tears falling from his eyes.

To see the powerful weep is a lesson in humility.

Moved, I reached out and touched his arm. "You did not fail," I whispered.

For a moment, Moco Jack lifted his eyes, as if to see who had spoken. In that instant he gazed at me, a deep, soulful regard. Yet he made no reply to my words, but looked down again.

The *Owners Goodwill* sailed on to America and I, perhaps for the first true time, began to consider what my life would be—a slave—under the absolute authority of a master for seven years. If powerful Moco Jack could be so suppressed, how could I survive?

I clutched that bit of Charity's lace and renewed my

vow that I would never cease my search for freedom and her. Let others succumb to tyranny, not I. Was I not a freeborn Englishman—or, at least, an English boy?

How brave the boast.

You may judge for yourself if I stayed true.

CHAPTER TEN

A Small Chapter in Which a Huge Question Is Asked.

The *Owners Goodwill* sailed on without encountering more storms. My mess, however, was reduced to five men, because, to my unlimited shock and horror, I woke one morning to find that I was chained to a corpse: my messmate Rufus Caulwell, the man who had told me about swamps.

I had no knowledge as to why the poor fellow perished. It could have been for many reasons, though not because of any singular mistreatment on the ship. We all were treated in a similar brutal fashion, save Moco Jack, who was abused the worst.

I did recall that this Mr. Caulwell had a wife and babes in London. His terrible crime, you may recall, was trying to feed them. As I gazed upon his lifeless, shrunken features, I had little doubt that his family would never know his fate.

Would they, nonetheless, wait for him?

It is common to say that we are often ignorant of what the future may hold for us. But I believe we may be just as ignorant about what has already occurred. We wait for someone to come, who never can, and cling to a hope that such and such might happen, when circumstances have already (without our knowledge) destroyed any chance.

That I, so young, was shackled to death struck me as a painful symbol for my world: bad enough that the young are by law bound to those who are old. Youth are also restrained even by those who have passed away, restricted by their antique teachings, habits, and laws, none of which we helped construct. Thus youth is shackled to a world constructed by the old and dead.

Such were my dark thoughts while it was my dreadfulness to remain bound to the dead man for some long hours. It remained that way until our daily food was provided and the first mate discovered the corpse. Only then was the late, lamentable Mr. Caulwell hauled away, fed, I suppose, to the ever-hungry sea. Nor should you think the dead man's rations were shared among those who remained alive. It was not to be so.

Would this miserable voyage ever end?

CHAPTER ELEVEN

In Which a Momentous Change Takes Place.

More endless days brought the death of other felons who were swiftly tossed into the sea. No doubt, the sharks that followed in our wake feasted fine. Meanwhile, our food grew worse, ever ghastlier. But, after some three or four more weeks, things began to change for the better. Hatches were left open. While it remained cold, the air became fresher.

Then, one morning, there came a most uncommon call: "All felons on deck."

To our astonishment, the chains about our necks and those that bound us to our messmates were removed. We were required—scrawny and feeble as we were—to move about. We were also made to wash ourselves in seawater, a good thing. We were ordered to scrub down our deck with vinegar to rid the ship insofar as possible of pestilence and stench. From then on, every day we were allowed the freedom of the top deck for at least an hour and sometimes more.

I hasten to add that though unshackled we were always guarded by the crew, who were armed with charged pistols and cudgels.

Those who wore naught but rags, such as my own clothing, which had long been reduced to shreds, were given new (old) togs. We were provided with rough haircuts. Those who had beards (not I) were shaved. Most marvelous of all, we were offered more and somewhat better food. I dare say we grew healthier and our strength revived.

At first, this was a marvelous mystery to us all. Had Captain Krets repented of his harsh treatment and our captivity? Was the miracle of our salvation from the storm to be extended? Were these changes part of a sudden shift to some Christian compassion?

"Please, sir," I asked one of the crew, "why is the captain showing such kindness?"

"Nothing to do with kindness," was the explanation. "You need to look good for the buyers."

"Sir?"

"So you may be bought for a better price."

A revelation. We were being treated the way drovers fatten cattle to bring them to market; I would be considered no more than a dumb beast. When we were sold the ship would gain a better profit.

CHAPTER TWELVE

My Arrival in the New World.

We were on deck, and the *Owners Goodwill* was still sailing westward before a steady wind, when the first mate called out, "Who among you can write?"

A few of us raised hands.

The captain looked about and pointed to me. "Come along, you," he commanded. I suspect he chose me because he assumed a boy was most manageable.

He led me into his own quarters, at the stern of the ship, where I had never been before. The cabin had fine furniture, along with racks of drink, chests full of food, dried fish and peas, oatmeal and, from the look of it, pickled meats. Captain Krets had—like the sharks that followed in our wake—eaten well during our voyage.

He placed a chair before a small desk and bid me to

be seated. A writing quill, a pot of ink, paper, plus blotting sand, were set before me.

"Write out a ledger. Each convict will be required to give his name, age, sentence, and any skillfulness that he might have mastered in England."

Accordingly, my fellow convicts were lined up outside the entryway and called in one by one. I wrote down all the required information. The first name I put in was my own, and as for my skills, I wrote, "Writing and reading." I did so in an excellent chancery hand, thinking that perhaps my penmanship would help me secure a good buyer. As I remembered from my school days: "Who 'ere has a good hand has a hand up."

As I continued to fill the book with descriptions of my fellow felons, I learned that most of us had no particular skills, but there was a nail maker, a baker's apprentice, a mason.

I gave the completed papers to the captain for a use I shall soon disclose.

When we were perhaps some seventy-five miles from the land I began to smell the enchanting incense of pine trees. It was a revelation. Though I had spent my whole life in this world taking little notice of its smells, other than the foulness of London, when that sweet whiff of America's vast forests came unto me, I knew it for what it was: land—earth—and was much upstirred by it. As sailors oft say, the fouler the sea the sweeter the shore.

Leafy branches floated in the water. A bird flew by and a member of the crew told me it was a "wild goose," a land bird.

Two days later came the cry "Land ho! Land ho!" from a seaman perched high in the yards above, someone no doubt eager to claim the captain's prize (two shillings) for being the first to sight the shore.

We felons, having the momentary freedom of the deck (ignoring for the moment the armed crew), lined the rails to gain our first glimpse of fabulous America. Of course, we were jubilant to be alive and see it. How soon did the terrors of sea voyaging (and that frightful tempest) evaporate. All the same, a moment's thought informed me (at least) that I was gaining a view of my vast new prison.

The talk, as we looked on, was for the most part nervous questions and uninformed answers.

"Do you think it will be crowded like London?"

"Nay. A wilderness."

"And who might be living there? People such as we know?"

"I assure you, mostly barbarians."

"Will they meet us with kindness or contempt, do you think?"

"They can't be worse than the captain."

Since our ignorance was total we looked upon the coast with a mix of dread and delight.

The *Owners Goodwill* tacked back and forth, until our new sails filled with propitious winds, after which we were able to sail north between Cape Henry and Cape Charles and entered a vast bay.

"What do they call this place?" I asked an older member of the crew.

"Chesapeake."

I recalled hearing that word along the quays of Melcombe Regis. "Does the word mean anything?"

"Indian word. 'Great water.' Goes straight north."

Whether true or not, I had no idea, but the water was wide. From the wooded forests that edged the bay—both shores—it was some twenty miles across. The bay was calm and full of islands, large and small. Along the jagged coasts were multiple inlets, as well as true rivers flowing into the great water.

Pods of porpoises wantoned about our ship, while the air was aflutter with birds that bore feathers of many hues. Large fish jumped clear from the water and splashed down again as if to give us joy for our safe arrival.

It was wild, beautiful, and full of freedom, unlike us.

We sailed deeper into the bay, and soon learned that our destination was the port of Annapolis, more than a hundred miles beyond the bay's entrance. The port was situated at the end of a peninsula, along what—as we were told—was the Severn River.

Near to this Annapolis a few other ships were tied up to what appeared to be a quay—what I learned the Americans call a "wharf." Standing off, our sails were reefed, and our anchor dropped with a loud splash. When it held, we swung round with a pleasing groan, rather like a deep sigh of relief.

There were some rattles of rigging, and then we ceased to move. Though we stood away from the land, there was no doubt: We had arrived in America. Seagulls flew about us, providing a squawking welcome. Or perhaps they were warning us.

Most miraculous of all, although thousands of miles from my home, I was still alive. I had survived.

A sailor told us it was the month of March. A calendar means a future. Of course, that future was as yet all unknown and dreaded. Indeed, I should have heeded the gulls.

America

CHAPTER THIRTEEN

In Which I Reach America.

I t took but a glance for me to see that Annapolis (named for England's late Good Queen Anne when she was yet a princess) was nothing like the monstrous city of London. Indeed, Annapolis had far fewer buildings than my own small English town, Melcombe Regis. Nonetheless, the captain informed us that this community was the seat of government for Maryland's royal colony. He was further pleased to claim that more people came to America through this port than any other. What I gathered from his words was that Charity might well be here. That thrilled me, and I took to gazing at the town as if I might see her. When that proved impossible, I took to wondering how I might find her.

As we remained anchored, a small boat rowed to where we were, perhaps some fifty yards from shore. In the boat were two oarsmen and a gentleman, for so he was dressed, including a wig, three-corner hat, jacket, lace, and boots—though perhaps less fancy than I had witnessed in London.

We dropped a rope ladder and this man—he was what they called a landwaiter, a customs official—came aboard to be met by our Captain Krets. I was unable to hear the words they spoke to each other, but from a distance, their discourse seemed casual and regular. The captain presented the man with some papers, which looked like legal documents.

I would learn that Captain Krets was providing official papers, which informed this landwaiter that he had legally brought a shipload of convicts and was prepared to sell them to those free citizens of Maryland and Virginia who wished to own servants.

No doubt—as the law required—he also spoke of the storm, and thereby sought to free himself of charges for damage and loss of cargo, sailors, and convicts. In short, his profits came from his hand. His losses came from God. Thus, the true religion of England.

At one point a gust of wind lifted the gentleman's wig. He managed to grab and replace it, but not before I saw that he was bald, a shaved head being a common defense against lice. It made me smile: There we were, thousands of miles from England, but lice were here too.

How comforting to know that North America and England shared this bond of little creatures.

Once the official left the ship, the captain called me to his cabin, sat me down, and had me write out the following advertisement:

Just arrived from London, a cargo of convicts in the ship Owners Goodwill, *Captain Elijah Krets: All felons in singular health and strength, ages twelve to forty-five. Among them are masons, a watchmaker, and a baker. Also, strong, healthy plantation laborers. They are to be sold for terms of seven to fourteen years for ready money or tobacco on board the said ship, now in Annapolis Dock.*

The first mate took the note into town, where it was to be printed and posted. In Maryland, having neither newspaper nor postal service, public notices were the sole way information was shared.

Meanwhile, I spent my time wondering a question I had not fully considered before: Who would buy me?

CHAPTER FOURTEEN

In Which I Have a Dangerous Desire.

Captain Krets spent the next two days working to gloss us convicts so as to make us as sellable as possible. The higher the price he could gain, and the quicker that sale took place, the more profitable for the *Owners Goodwill* and the London gentlemen who had invested in her. After all, transporting convicts was a business, and the object of business is to make money. That the captain was trafficking in people made no difference to him.

Most important, this was the time that each of us had an iron collar bolted to our necks to mark us as convicts. The collar was a rough circlet of gray iron—called a "pothook," for reasons I didn't know. Though hard and strong, it could be bent open and closed round our necks by two strong crewmen. The ends were fastened shut with a bent-over nail by a third.

For me, so young and a rather small neck, the collar fitted loosely and merely chafed. For others of bigger size, it was a painful choker. This collar served as both a badge of felonry and a sign: If we ran away, we would, on sight, be identified as escapee convicts. It also made it easy to lead us about and treat us as tethered beasts.

As we waited and prepared, another ship came in. She was a slaver, with a large cargo of Negro men, women, and children, whom I could see quite plainly. All the passengers were in chains. I guessed she came direct from Africa.

Buyers appeared and took off great numbers of those unfortunate souls. Families must have been separated for there were horrendous cries and shrieks of grief. These people, I reminded myself, were to be owned by their purchasers not for seven years, like me, but for their entire lives.

Did it make me feel better that my enslavement was for mere years? No, but let it be said that my pity for them was the greater. I might become free. They would never return to their own land and lives. I lived with a small sliver of hope. They had none. How could they bear it? Could they ever find a way to escape? Did they know of that fairy-tale swamp?

During the night before our own sale took place we unchained convicts sat with one another out of habit, like companions taking leave before a long journey.

"I'll pray tonight for a soft master," said one Mr. Kelly.

"I'm just praying I can serve out my time and be alive," was Mr. Dybas's contribution.

An older man, a Mr. Honeycutt, said, "This is my second time. I was lucky to the first. An easy master, God protect him. But I promise you're more likely to find hardness. These masters can squeeze water from rocks."

"Who are these masters?" I asked.

The same Mr. Honeycutt answered, "Of each hundred men who live about these plantations, only some twenty-five are free. The rest are slaves, indentured servants, or convicts like us. It's free men who buy us."

This caused me to recall another of my father's beliefs: "I will have no servants. It demeans both master and servant." Yet it appeared that I was about to enter a world of few masters and many servants. What kind of land was it, I wondered, this Maryland, which had such a society?

"Do all the colonies have slaves and convict labor?" I asked.

"All," was the chorused answer.

"So if you try to run off," cautioned a new voice, "or go against your master, you can't get away. You'll be punished and your bondage time lengthened."

"Never mind masters," called out another. "They say the summer heat alone here will kill you."

Among my mess there were some who vowed that we would meet again (no one said where, when, or how) as well as what they would do upon returning to England. One man wondered if his parents would recall him when he went back. Another pondered if his lap kid would acknowledge him so many years hence.

To sit among men who were about to be enslaved was to share their fear and despair. As my messmates talked about dismal futures, I listened until dejection dropped upon me like a funeral shroud. Beyond hating to hear their dire predictions, I was much unnerved. How would I ever endure? No wonder that when night came I tried to sleep but could do little more than stare into the darkness, unable to see any light on the ship or in my life.

I had faded into a slumber—I have no idea the hour—when I felt a touch. I opened my eyes. It was Moco Jack. He had edged close, and now whispered into my ear, "Oliver. Are you awake?"

"I think so," I said, though drowsy.

"What mind-sights have you?"

"I . . . I keep wondering what will become of me."

"Aye, when I think where we're going I worry much. But I don't intend to let them determine my life."

I was surprised that Moco Jack had spoken, much less that he had chosen to say such a thing to me.

"What do you mean?" I said.

In a voice barely above a murmur, he said, "I'm going to escape."

That flung off my drowsiness. "How?" I said, sitting up.

"I'm going to swim to shore," said Moco Jack. "For once, we're unchained and the land is close enough."

I felt a surge of upstirring. Hardly thinking, I blurted out, "Will you take me with you?"

"Do you swim?"

"No, sir," I replied. Not only did I lack swimming skills but during my days in Melcombe Regis we considered swimming—that is, floating on the water—a form of witchcraft. Neither I nor any of my friends, though we lived on the edge of the sea, could swim.

"Can you swim?" I inquired.

"I can," said Moco Jack. "But when they find me gone, I'll trust you'll not reveal how I got away."

"No, sir. Be sure, I won't. But . . . can't you take me with you?"

Moco Jack studied me. Then he said, "I wouldn't offer the same to a man my size, but you're slight. If you truly want to come, I'm strong enough to carry you with me."

"Would you?" I whispered, much upstirred.

"You were kind to me before when I was defeated."

"When will you go?" I said, all abubble.

"Before dawn," he went on in an even softer voice,

"the watch will be sleepy. I'll take to the water then. You can leap with me. You'll sink some but I'll catch you up and carry you through. Mind, the water will be cold. Are you game?"

I nodded. "Once on land, where will you go?"

"Wherever I can get my freedom. Just know," Moco Jack cautioned, "it will go hard for us if we are caught." He put a hand to his iron collar by way of a reminder. "Are you sure you wish to try?"

I suppose it was all the dreadful talk I had heard about the life on land that awaited me, which put me in a mind to agree. There I was, a twelve-year-old confronting seven years of hard labor under the hand—believing my messmates—of an unknown and most likely severe master. I fingered my iron collar. Though loose, it was already hateful.

Would it not, I thought, be far better to escape, gain my liberty, and seek my sister, Charity? Had I not resolved to resist authority? Did I not want to be brave?

I barely hesitated. "If you're willing to take me," I said, "I'll go."

"Then God be with us," whispered Moco Jack, giving me a pat. "Now, get some rest. You'll have need. I'll wake you when I'm ready." He crept away and lay down as if to sleep.

I found it hard to believe Moco Jack would try to do as

he said, or that I had asked to go with him. But my willing thought was thus: I was being given the choice between slavery and freedom. How could I choose anything but liberty?

I would leap from the ship.

CHAPTER FIFTEEN

The Escape and What Came of It.

I struggled to stay awake, but since youth and sleep are as hard to pry apart as a wet knot, I folded into slumbers.

Early morning, I felt a poke, which bestirred me to full wakefulness. Moco Jack was bending over me like a crouching spider. I got up quickly, albeit silently. Then we crept toward the steps, moving so as to avoid sleeping convicts.

With Moco Jack in the lead, going slowly, we reached the companionway. Once atop the steps, he lifted his head up and surveyed the open deck.

"Safe," he called down in a shushing whisper. "Now, quick," he added, and moved farther up.

Heart pounding, I followed him, and in moments stood next to him upon the main deck. Remembering what I was about to do—leap to liberty—I was grateful that Moco Jack, at least, knew what to do.

It was not entirely dark but rather that iron gray that precedes the dawn. The *Owners Goodwill* lay easy on her anchor, with only an occasional small slap of water against the hull, and now and again a creak of wood, like a rasping, rusty hinge, an open door.

I looked up. Masts and spars appeared as so many open hands and fingers. Sails were furled. In the higher sky were naught but a few fading stars and a small slip of moon streaked by speeding clouds that afforded us more obscurity. A gull on the top rail had its head tucked into its feathers—still asleep. The world appeared utterly peaceable. As far as I could tell, we were alone, unobserved and all but free. Can you doubt I felt a throb of joy?

Once on deck, Moco Jack, in a crouch, paused to peer about. I believed he was deciding the side of the ship from which to leap—that is to say, the side closest to shore. A few yards might make a mortal difference. His mind made up, he crept toward the port side, stopped, turned, and made a beckoning gesture.

For my part, I took a step to follow when, out of the edge of my eye, I observed movement at the bow of the ship. Alarmed, I halted and stared at the spot, but saw nothing.

Even so it was enough to make me uncertain and hold back. But as Moco Jack continued to move with great care toward the top rail, I ventured another step, only to yet again see movement near the bow. This time, however, someone stood up.

Captain Krets.

I also saw a glint of metal, which informed me the captain had a pistol in his hand. His face was turned toward Moco Jack, not me.

I was just about to call out, when the captain himself cried, "Halt."

"Moco Jack," I shouted. "We're undone."

Not for a moment did Moco Jack hesitate. He sprang forward and jumped upon the rail. There he perched, his slender body teetering, as if about to fly.

Captain Krets extended his arm, so that the pistol was now aimed right at my friend.

Miss fire, miss fire, I prayed.

Four things seemed to happen at once: Moco Jack leaped toward the water. With a red spurt of flame, the gun fired. There was a loud *bang*. I heard a splash. Was my friend dead or alive? Was he sinking or swimming?

I remained where I was only long enough to see the captain rush to the side of the ship and peer over, as he worked hard to reload his gun. I all but dropped down the steps to the lower deck and scrambled to my regular place. Once there, I flung myself down and pretended motionless sleep, though my wide-awake heart was galloping.

Had Moco Jack escaped? Had the captain heard me call out?

As I lay there, another pistol shot exploded. I could only assume it was the captain firing at Moco Jack. Did that bode well or ill? I could not know.

Then, silence. Silence absolute. All I knew was that Moco Jack was gone. But was he free or dead? Perhaps merely wounded. Or bleeding to death. I had no knowledge. Whether he had gained his freedom or his God, I had no answer.

Within moments—as I continued to lie still, pretending to be asleep—someone, perhaps two, descended to the lower deck. I kept my eyes closed, but sensed a shining light. I supposed it was the captain and first mate surveying the convicts, perhaps counting us, trying to see if any other men were gone. At one point I was sure they were standing next to me. I held my breath and refrained from moving.

After some long while, the captain and the mate withdrew, leaving our deck in darkness. I heard the hatchway slam shut. No doubt double bolted. I stayed where I was, continuing to wonder as to Moco Jack's fate.

Had he escaped? Had he been killed? Had I lost my chance for freedom?

When more time passed, and nothing happened, or sounded, I considered going up to the deck and doing what my friend had done. But the hatchway was closed, probably locked, and that witching art of swimming was beyond me. To escape in that fashion was to drown. There would be no escape for me. Not then. All I could do was resolve to learn the skill of swimming and make use of it if another such opportunity arose.

Morning came, and Moco Jack was discovered to be missing but no more than a small flutter was made by the crew. At first naught was said of the pistol shots and what came of them. There were whispers among us felons, but as promised I pleaded ignorance.

Later that morning, the captain lined us convicts up in preparation for buyers to come aboard.

"I wish to inform you," the captain proclaimed, "that Moco Jack attempted to escape, was shot, wounded, caught, and taken ashore: that by his actions he has extended his term of transportation from seven years to fourteen. Let that be an example to you all."

I had to wonder: Did the captain tell the truth? My fervent wish was that Moco Jack had gained his freedom. But I had no way of learning. No more than I knew if I would ever find Charity.

Oh, how we yearn for outright endings, good or bad. But alas, I have learned that life is more often a list of questions, with answers that are rarely yes or no if given at all. The world is full of maybe, perhaps, and I don't know. I would never learn the fate of Moco Jack.

What I did learn for certain was this: A man like the captain never allows the notion to get about that someone made his way to freedom. It would give others the idea of escaping. Tyranny will always deny the smallest possibility of liberty and thereby reduce the resolve of those who seek it.

I had little time to think such big thoughts, however, because in a brief while the buyers were to come aboard.

Moco Jack—dead or alive—was, in some fashion, free no matter what the captain said. I was alive but about to be sold.

CHAPTER SIXTEEN

In Which We Are Given Advice How to Sell Ourselves.

I t was mid-morning when four or perhaps five small dories, propelled by sailors with oars, approached the *Owners Goodwill*. Ropes were dropped and gathered so that our ship was towed to a wooden quay. This quay poked any number of yards into the town itself, a kind of inlet, round which clustered some modest wooden buildings. A few other boats, sloops and the like, all rather small, were also at the wharf. For the first time, I also observed what I would come to know as a canoe. Other, bigger boats were being loaded with large round barrel-like containers, pushed up gangways by Negroes, slaves, I presumed.

The ropes that were used to haul the *Owners Goodwill* were the same that warped the ship against the quay and held us fast. Long wooden planks were laid down from our ship to give people easy access.

Before the ship was towed in, we prisoners had been chained one to another, with particular use of the iron collars that had been fastened round our necks. Then we were arranged in six lines of thirteen men, with a three-foot space between rows.

The crew had been armed with pistols, muskets, and cudgels and stood guard over us. Whether this was the normal practice, or was done because of Moco Jack's escape (or death), we were not told.

Captain Krets came forward and addressed us.

"Pay heed. The buyers will be coming aboard soon. You shall answer their questions and oblige yourself to their close inspection. It will be much to your advantage to respond to them with such honesty as you still have, courtesy if it exists, and whatever good humor remains within you. It is for them to choose or not choose to purchase you. You have no voice in the matter. You have no right to ask anything.

"Be further advised," continued the captain, "if you are not bought and taken away, I shall not free you or bring you back to England, where you would only be hanged. Rather, you will become the property of Annapolis and placed in their jail. Therefore, it shall profit me nothing to keep you on this ship. Quite the contrary. If you touch land—unbought—you belong to this town. In all probability, you'll rot to death. Your fate, then, is in your own smutted hands. It will be to your great advantage to sell yourself. A smile might help."

Not so different, I thought, from my father's cynical advice: "To get on you must mask your heart with false smiles."

"And," continued the captain, "be further advised that anyone who attempts to break free shall immediately be hanged from the spars." Captain Krets actually smiled. "I wish you all good fortune and a future that will reward you for your honest labor. God save King George."

Once these kind, helpful, and patriotic words were spoken, the buyers were allowed to come on board.

CHAPTER SEVENTEEN

In Which I Am Offered for Sale and What Came of It.

As the day wore on, perhaps fifty or so buyers came aboard. Who were they? In the first instance, they were almost all men, there being but one woman among them. To my best guess, they ranged in age from their twenties to some as ancient as sixty.

Beyond that it was hard for me to know what manner of men and woman they were, their station in life, much less their occupations. One or two of the men—by London fashion—appeared to be gentlemen of wealth, complete with fine powdered wigs, silk stockings and jackets with bright silver buttons, and buckles on their shoes.

Most of the buyers, however, seemed to be of the middling sort and dressed as tradesmen, or farmers, with simple jackets, boots, and black slouch hats. A few seemed poorer. Nonetheless, all were there to purchase us.

At the gangway, at the point where they stepped upon the ship, these buyers were met by the first mate. I could hear the buyers telling him the kind of skill they desired, say a carpenter or chandler. Mr. Babington consulted the ledger I had written up, then pointed out convicts that met a particular need. These buyers also partook of a large bowl of punch the captain had set out, so as to make them more affable. Then they began to saunter up and down the convict lines, examining us as if we were so many dumb beasts.

I studied their faces and was struck how little emotion they showed as they went about purchasing people.

Who, I wondered, would want a boy that could read and write? Would my master be kind or cruel? Would I live out my term, or die?

First to be bought were men with specific skills, such as masons and farriers. These folks commanded the highest price—twenty pounds a man—after much bargaining twixt shoppers and the captain. Then the more common laborers were sold, and I judged their prices—eight pounds—were set by strength, health, and age.

It was not—for the most part—actual money that was used to purchase us so much as signed promissory notes of tobacco. It appeared that in Maryland, the tobacco leaf was more often used for currency than true money, which was valued at whatever was the sot-weed's (as tobacco was called) current market price.

As the day wore on, more and more convicts were led away to servitude. Although the older ones did not go for high sums, most of the buyers did not even glance at me before passing on. Since I was rather small for my years, I suspected most considered me too young, perhaps too cheerful in appearance, to do such scabrous tasks as they had in mind. It was hard, durable labor they were wanting, not a smiling boy.

I was considered. Prospective buyers peered into my face, perhaps looking for signs of the pox. Sometimes they asked me to open my mouth so as to search my teeth to be sure I had them. (A fair number of my fellow felons did not.) They smelled my breath to sense if I contained any rottenness within. They pinched my arms to judge such strength as I had—or had not. Some counted my fingers. A few bid me to walk about to see if I limped or dragged a foot.

This prodding inquisition was all about my physical self. They would have done as much for a cow. There was little interest in me, Oliver Cromwell Pitts. It was as if I, the mindful person, was without value, naught but bone and muscle. And, let me admit, I had little of that.

While now this frail and uneducated man, now that dull and undexterous fellow was led away, I continued to be ignored. As the day went on, there began to grow in my mind the captain's threat: that if I were not acquired, I would be left to rot in the local jail. It is perhaps repellent to admit, but being disregarded—not being bought—made me feel bad. Since the thought of escaping was forever in my mind, I told myself it would be far better to be with a person than in prison.

As the day wore on, I wanted to be bought. How perverse.

At last someone—the sole woman among the buyers—stopped to consider me. With her goodly face and intelligent looks, I thought she would not be harsh, and decided I wanted her to buy me.

She was, I judged, of middle age, with bits of stray gray hair dangling from her cap. She wore a linen shift, over which was a long bodice, then over all an apron. On her feet were decent leather shoes suggesting modest means.

I always had what my sister had chosen to call an impish, merry face. Because of my pleasing looks people often had taken a protective attitude toward me. Surely—I thought—a woman would care for someone such as me, a tender youth. There must be some mothering in her. How nice, I allowed myself to think—I who had lost my mother when I was born—to regain another.

I therefore endeavored to put on my sweetest smile, tried to fill my eyes with gratitude, and flung all the charms that God gave me upon this woman.

With a most solemn bearing, she studied me awhile and then began to ask questions:

"Have you had any illness, boy?"

"No, madam."

"How long is your sentence?"

"Seven years, madam."

"What is your name?"

"Oliver Cromwell Pitts."

"A horrid name," she said. "At least, I presume, a Protestant. Just know we want no popish folk, Quakers, or Jews here. Where do you come from?"

"England. Melcombe Regis on the Dorset coast."

"How old are you?"

"Twelve years."

"You look younger."

"I speak true, madam."

"What was your crime?"

"I took money from a wrecked ship, madam."

"How much?"

"Twenty-three shillings, madam."

She stiffened. "Despite your age, a true rogue."

I shuddered. This was not what I had expected.

"Have you any trade?" she asked.

That question delighted me for I assumed I had an answer that would serve her and me. "I attended school," I said, "and was apprenticed to a lawyer, madam." (I did not reveal that the lawyer was my father.) "I can read and write. And I can do numbers, madam."

"Truly?" Her look was drenched in doubt.

"Yes, madam."

She did not smile. Rather, she frowned. "You had best learn," she said, "that the wisest servant has the dumbest mind. Do you have family?"

"A father and a sister."

"And where are they?"

"I last saw my father in London, madam. I have no idea where my sister is."

I held back that Charity was transported.

The woman gazed at me as if trying to make up her mind. At last she said, "I fear you would have a bad influence on my children."

She passed on and bought a fellow who was a confessed murderer.

So much for our mutual judgment of people.

CHAPTER EIGHTEEN

In Which My Hope Darkens and the Reader Is Offered a Warning.

As the sky turned gloomy, so did my hopes. Of all the felons, I alone had not been purchased. Indeed, it was not long before even the crew departed from the *Owners Goodwill*. How dreadful to say it: remembering the captain's warning that if I was not sold I would rot to death in a jail, I envied my fellow convicts.

Imagine if you will: A young convict boy whom no one wants (least of all his own country) stands solitary on a ship's deserted deck, near the shore of an unknown land countless miles from his home. No family to comfort me. No friend. The only connection to my kin was a bit of my sister's lace, hidden in the bottom of my pocket.

There was, moreover, an iron collar round my neck—

emblem of felony and servitude. I had been beneath the sun all day. Having been given nothing to eat, I was famished.

As I stood there, forlorn and forsaken, I observed Captain Krets and the first mate in close conference. Their continual glances in my direction left me in little doubt that it was I about whom they were talking.

At length Mr. Babington came to me and said, "Come along, boy." By way of particular persuasion, he held a pistol in his hand. For a terrible moment, I thought he was going to execute me, and thereby be rid of his encumbrance. Instead, he linked a rope leash—some six feet in length—to my iron collar and led me down the gangway to the wharf.

After nine weeks of ocean voyaging, I bid a rueful farewell to the *Owners Goodwill*, and for the first time set my foot upon the new world. I cannot tell you the precise date, but the temperature was rather mild, the air soft and moist: spring, the season of hope. In my heart, it might as well have been winter for what I was thinking; would I ever regain my liberty?

At the foot of the gangway was a man, whom I recognized as the government official who had first come upon our ship when we reached Annapolis.

The first mate told me to stand fast while he went to

confer with this gentleman. As I stood waiting, my bare feet experienced the solidity of earth, which, to my surprise, I had quite forgotten. It was odd to stand upon a surface that remained steady beneath my feet, free from the ship's pitch and roll.

For a few moments, Mr. Babington and the government man conferred in small voices after which the first mate gave my rope leash to this man. Without so much as a farewell nod or a backward glance, the first mate left me and returned to the *Owners Goodwill*. I saw neither ship nor man again. Amazingly, I felt a pang of loss, clinging to the bad I knew, so fearful was I of the unknown.

The government man considered me with a baleful gaze that informed me I was an unwelcome problem. With no courtesy, he tugged the leash and said, "Come along."

"Please, sir," I said, "where am I going?"

"Jail," was the brusque reply, and he held up a large key as if that provided proof of his word. Then he gave a snap to the leash, wrenching my neck. Having no choice, I moved. In short, my admittance to this new world, this new life, this new America, was like a tethered dog.

A fair warning: There are some, upon reading the first volume of my memoirs, who commented upon my cheery, optimistic character in the face of all hardships. From this point on, let me warn you that the kind of difficulties I was about to endure left little room for wit or winsomeness. That said, I beg you not to abandon me, but travel by my side until the end—no matter where it might be.

CHAPTER NINETEEN

In Which I Pass Through Annapolis at the End of a Leash.

The Annapolis official walked before me saying nothing, which at least afforded me a closer view of the world into which I'd been brought. I told myself to pay particular attention so that if I managed to break free, I'd know my way about.

A glance informed me that I could not call Annapolis a true city. Captain Krets had told us that more persons came to America through this part than any other. Even so, to my eyes Annapolis was merely a village, though it was the chief town of the royal colony, the seat of its government. My own Melcombe Regis had a population of four thousand. Annapolis appeared to have hardly more than six hundred. Cows and pigs wandered about with great freedom—surely more than my own. Was all of America, I mused, so void of people?

The quay where we had arrived was part of a rectangular cove set right into the town. At the head of the inlet was a small marketplace. Beyond, the community was dominated by the high steeple of a church. There couldn't have been more than a hundred buildings in all. While most were wooden houses—built of a reddish timber, which I would learn was from local cypress tree—a few were brick. Most buildings were one-story structures set on irregular stone foundations with brick chimneys at the gabled roof ends. The streets, angled in irregular fashion, were all unpaved.

Yes, I sensed newness, whereas Melcombe Regis was old. But that same newness suggested a lack of society as I had known it.

The town had hills—low ones—so that, being built on a peninsula, I could see water no matter where I was. At the town's highest point was an elegant two-story brick building set within a circle. As I would learn, it was what they called the Government House.

Close by that structure was St. Anne's Church, also brick, set in another circle. It was sited somewhat lower than the Government House, though its steeple was the tallest point in town, topped as it was by a golden ball and weathervane.

Narrow streets radiated from these two circles, so plots of land were oddly shaped. Here and there were trees.

As we continued to walk, I studied the passersby. They were of all sorts, tradesmen, artisans, farmers, men and women both, dressed much as they would be in England. Most were white, some were Negroes. No one paid me any heed. Now and again, I did see children. They (unlike their elders) stared at me, as if perplexed by the sight of a boy led by a leash.

As ever, Charity was never far from my thoughts, so I was looking for her. Since I had been informed that most transported felons were sent from England to Annapolis, why not Charity?

I did not truly expect to see my sister, but then again, as far as I knew, she could be anywhere, assuming she had lived through her voyage.

Alas, I didn't spy her.

I was led through the whole town on what I would learn was Church Street, going past St. Anne's, then north until we came upon a small stone box of a building. No more than twenty feet to a side, it appeared to be a dungeon, built to withstand my ferocity. It had one small window, with crisscrossing rusty bars and a narrow wooden door, studded with nails. It suggested much to me about America that the strongest structure I had yet observed was a jail.

My guardian applied the key to the door, unlocked it, and pulled it open. Seeing the dismal hole that yawned before me, I was reluctant to go farther.

"Get within," was the blunt order.

"Please, sir, how long will I stay? Will I be fed? Will anyone come and fetch me?"

"No insolent questions," returned the man. "Get."

Having no choice, I did as I was told, and stepped into the small room. Well squared, it had some old straw heaped upon the hard dirt floor. There was a little, barred window and a foul-smelling wooden bucket; nothing else. All was dull and getting darker.

Even as I, quite dispirited, stood there and looked about, the Annapolis man took my leash and affixed it with a lock to a ring that was attached to a stone wall.

Without so much as a farewell, the man left, slamming the door behind him. The sprightly snap of a closing lock followed.

Once again, I was in a jail.

CHAPTER TWENTY

The Joys of Being in America.

I f you have read the first part of my memoirs, you know that, although young, I had already been confined multiple times. Did that mean that I, accustomed to such places, enjoyed a sense of ease? Not to the smallest degree. Rather, I bestirred myself by trying to discover yet once again if I could escape.

I began by trying to undo my leash, first from my neck, then from the wall. No success. I attempted to take off my iron collar. I could not. I also struggled with the door. It held tight. I even applied myself to the window, pulling upon each of the six rusty bars in turn. They proved unmovable. In such light as remained and my leash allowed, I went round the perimeter of the cell, kicking the foundation stones, now and again feeling one, in hopes it might be loose. None were.

In short, all my efforts proved useless. At least the rope was long enough so that I had some freedom of movement, though no true freedom.

Feeling altogether mumpish, I gathered some of the rotten straw into a pile, so as to make a softer spot on the solid earth floor, and sat down, the leash slack, my back pressed against the cold and jagged stone wall. I drew up my knees, draped arms and hands over them, and worked hard to convince myself I was better off than I had been on the convict ship; I was alive, I told myself, and that having life meant hope remained.

Nonetheless, it was all too clear to me that I had no way of absconding, nor did I have any idea how long I would be confined. Would I even be remembered? Or would I be forgotten, left to languish and die in this small, barren place, which already felt like a tomb? Would I, in Captain Krets's vivid words, which grew in my thoughts, be left to rot?

I had been in a London jail. Now I was in an American one. They were thousands of miles apart. How much the same. Misery has no geography.

I scratched myself. I mussed my hair. Rubbed my face. I let my mind wander over all that had led me to such a place and predicament. Now and again I fingered Charity's lace.

There was this difference: I had been imprisoned

before, but this was the first time I was alone. I wanted to cry, but discovered that I was empty of emotions. My ordeal had drained me of tears. I, who had been accused of robbery, had been robbed of my heart.

Those who haven't had the horror of being imprisoned cannot understand. To protect oneself against the gross experience, a convict imprisons his or her own emotions; seals them away like an oyster uses an impenetrable shell to protect its soft innards. Thus, I sat in a state of rigid numbness, such that it might well be called that appalling word—bedeaded.

A thief steals but coins. A prison steals hope.

How long I remained there with such an empty, desolate spirit, I cannot say. At some point, the darkness deepening along with my despair, my mind blank, my heart drained of courage, my stomach arumble with emptiness, I heard the fall of steps without. Startled, I looked and beheld light beneath the door's lower edge.

Someone was approaching.

As the door swung open I jumped up.

A man stepped forward. In one hand, he held a lit lantern. In his other was a lifted pistol. My instant thought was, I am about to be murdered.

CHAPTER TWENTY-ONE

In Which I Greet an Astonishing Visitor.

The light from this man's lantern threw shadows on his dirty and ill-shaved face, so as to give him an evil cast. No wig was on his head. Rather, his jumbled, dark hair was long enough so that it dangled below his shoulders. Around his neck was a stained cloth, and his tawdry jacket was partly torn with buttons missing. Boots were patched. And of course, there was that cocked pistol.

If ever anyone looked to be an assassin, it was this man.

He took three steps into the cell, and with a booted foot, crudely kicked the door shut behind him. Not that he ever took his eyes from me. On the contrary: Holding up his lantern, while pointing his pistol at my chest, he studied me with such hostile eyes that I felt obliged to retreat into a corner. My heart throbbed at a frantic rate.

The man said nothing. Instead, he continued to consider me for long, wordless moments, as if making up his mind whether to shoot me or not. Or—I thought—he was praying for forgiveness for the dastardly deed he was about to do.

Next I heard a puff of breath, as if to register surprise. When he spoke, he said, "You're just a boy."

Most peculiar, his words and voice sounded oddly familiar, and brought forward an indefinable memory of something similar said to me some time ago, which in the moment, I was powerless to recall.

This man, however, persisted in studying me with a deep, ruminating silence as if I were some ghost or spirit, even as I tried to grasp what seemed so familiar about him. Then his mouth took the shape of a near-perfect O. He started back, as if he had reason to fear me. What's more, he lowered his pistol and demanded, "What are you doing here? Have you come to hound me? Have you been sent by Mr. Wild?"

"Whom?"

"Jonathan Wild. England's infamous thief-taker."

I was mazed to hear the name. Mr. Wild was the principal criminal with whom I'd become ensnared in England. Indeed, it would be fair to say that it was Mr. Wild who brought about my transportation. Just to hear his name instilled fear.

"He has long arms," said the man. "Did he send you after me?"

Altogether baffled, I said, "Please, sir, I'm an unsold convict. Just transported from England. On my ship, I was the only one not purchased and therefore brought here."

My words instantly reduced the man's visible fright, but he continued to study me with something that suggested wonder. "You don't know me," he said. "Do you?"

"Should I?" I said.

"Melcombe Regis," said the man. "The old fort at the Narrows." Then he offered up an unexpected if somewhat toothless smile, shoved his pistol into his belt, and presented a kind of bow, his leg extended as if to present a satire on a gentleman.

It was as if light flooded into that small room: I did know him. "Mr. Sandys," I cried.

It was thus: When fleeing my English home— Melcombe Regis—so as to escape my father's enemies, I sought refuge in the old Narrows Fort. There I came upon this same Mr. Sandys who was hiding from the notorious Jonathan Wild.

What I learned then was that Mr. Sandys was a violent man, a self-confessed highwayman. He had done me (and others, no doubt) considerable harm. But—it is curious—a familiar face, far from home, is oft given a welcome whether deserved or not. Thus, to come upon him at such a place and time—in Annapolis—made me look upon him as a friend.

"But . . . but why are you here?" I cried.

"I trust you can recall my circumstance," he said, as if we were old friends sharing new gossip. "Being dogged by that hellhound Jonathan Wild, I was obliged to remove myself from England as fast as possible to get beyond his grasp. I searched for an agent, signed a bond—indentures. I trust you understand what that means: In exchange for passage to America I sold my labor. In my haste to flee, I boarded the first ship to depart.

"A fast voyage of six weeks brought me to this wretched place. Servants being scarce, I was purchased by this town, so now I'm a bonded servant to Annapolis. And will be so for four years.

"I've no end of chores. Night watchman for the town, sweeper at the court, and prison turnkey. I also feed prisoners and empty the bucket. It's a small town, but has two prisons, for this is a country swarming with villains and rogues."

He smirked as if all this was amusing.

"The gentry here, though they have no real knowledge of the law, become magistrates and justices of the peace. Protection of property is their prime concern. Let a man come onshore that displays the smallest knowledge of English law and he becomes a judge, with no qualms about ruling people guilty. Since I'm the one who puts offenders into the pillory and serves as town hangman, I'm kept busy." He paused and looked at me as if he were surprised all over again to discover me here.

"But how did you become a convict?" he inquired. "Did Mr. Wild impeach you?" He chuckled. "Did I not warn you about him?"

I provided a quick summary of all that had happened to me, leaving out my sister's tale.

Mr. Sandys listened, nodding now and again, sometimes laughing as if my history was highly entertaining. At other points, he frowned or shook his head at my plight.

At first I thought it was extraordinary that we should even meet again. But when I thought on it, there were ample reasons for such a reunion: Many ships from Melcombe Regis came direct to Annapolis, from where Sandys set off. The local population was scant. The list of his tasks fit his character all too well. How could I not come upon him?

When I had told my tale, he said, "You may consider yourself lucky to be alive. And you seem to have learned that for such as us, mercy and money, in the government's dictionary, are the same word."

"Then are you going to show me mercy and let me go?" I blurted. Thinking of him as my companion in hard treatment and worse luck, I spoke with an expectation that he would say yes.

"Let you go?" he echoed.

"Aren't we good friends?" I asked.

Sandys shook his head. "Nay, lad. I fear I'm duty-bound to my tasks. It would be worth my life to go against what I'm supposed to do with you. If I break the law—which is designed to keep you here—my own years in bondage would be much extended. I won't take the chance. I grant you, we are friends of misfortune, but we share more misfortune than friendship."

"Then why did you come to this place?" I asked.

"I was informed there was a new prisoner. I've brought food. It's my task."

"What will happen to me?" I cried.

He shrugged. "You'll stay till someone buys you."

"How long will that be?"

"I have no idea."

"But what if no one buys me?"

"They have a pauper's cemetery nearby. It won't cost you anything to be buried. Since grave-master is another of my tasks, I'll let you down easy."

As if to rehearse that moment, I slumped to the floor, my new-sprouted hopes squashed as quickly as they had grown.

Mr. Sandys contemplated me in silence. After some moments passed, he said, "I might do one thing for such a good friend." He grinned at the jest.

I looked up.

"Maryland wants laborers, which means there are always men about town in need of field hands. Instead of having you wait and suffer, I could seek out someone who might buy you."

"Would he?"

"I'm afraid boys your age are of sad use. You've little strength and tend to die quickly. But I could provide a good word for you, say you had prodigious power while always meek and obedient. If the price was low enough you might be bought."

I suppose I could have been more appreciative, but all I said was, "What would such a man require of me?"

"May I remind you, boy, that when a man is going to be hanged, the quality of rope that does the deed matters little. Shall I search out a buyer or no?"

"I'm willing," I allowed myself to say, uncertain if I was choosing wisely. I wondered, too, why was he being sympathetic to me? Was it the air in America? Because he had escaped from Mr. Wild? Regretful as to how he had once used me?

Mr. Sandys, as if construing my thoughts, said, "You

treated me well in England, so I feel obliged to return the favor. I assure you, boy, better to be sold than to remain here. But let me get you the bread I brought."

He briefly stepped out of the cell and returned with a loaf. He handed it to me with a smile. "Indian corn bread. Not as good as my mother's."

Though the bread was heavy and stale, I ate with hungry passion.

"Now then," said Sandys, "I have my other prison to look after."

"Will you truly seek out a man to purchase me?"

"You have my word that I'll try. Trust between thieves." He laughed. "Do you know I don't believe I ever learned your name."

"Oliver Cromwell Pitts."

"My honor, Master Pitts." He made his sardonic bow again, smiling as if he was amused by the absurdity of the situation. Then he was gone, the door locked behind him.

Only after he left did I realize I'd forgotten to request freedom from my rope. I remained little more than a tethered bird in a locked cage.

CHAPTER TWENTY-TWO

In Which I Seek (Once Again) to Escape.

I slept but poorly.

In the morning when I shook my head free of frowsiness and realized where I was, I woke poorly, too. My sole liberty was that I was able to use the wooden bucket to relieve myself. But to free one's bowels is not freedom, merely relief. Beyond that, I remained locked and chained. Full of despair, I waited, I knew not for whom.

But how do you wait for someone you don't know? Far worse, how do you wait when you are not even certain you wish to encounter the person who might come? And . . . what if, in the end, he doesn't come at all?

I shall tell you with conviction, that of all labors, waiting for the unknown—unable to guess if good or bad will happen—is surely one of the most exhausting things one can do.

Alas, I had no choice, none, so I remained in place half the day, long enough to despair of anyone coming. At times, I was certain no one would come and I thought I would starve to death. Other times, I went back to thinking of Mr. Sandys as a scoundrel. Or, feeling Charity's lace bit in hand, which was becoming ever more soiled and worn between my fingers, I wondered where she was and would I ever see her again. To be alone is to be crowded with thoughts.

At length, I told myself I really must make efforts to escape.

To that end, I first attacked the embedded wall knob to which my tether was attached. Since the knob stuck out from the wall I was able to grasp and wiggle it back and forth. After considerable time, the mortar began to loosen and eventually I managed to pull the knob from the wall, lock and all.

The leash, however, was still attached to my neck collar, which I could not remove. Still, I had made progress: I had gained the complete freedom of my cell.

Encouraged, I began to prod anew the stones with which the prison walls were built, testing to see if any were loose. Since I had all the time in the world, with nothing to lose and my freedom to gain, I worked diligently, trying stone after stone, ceiling to floor.

After considerable poking, prying, and pulling, I found

one stone—perhaps two feet above the ground—that wobbled slightly. My powers, dilapidated as they were, now came further alive and my fingers dug about, prying and pulling away at the stone.

To my great gratification, I was able to free the stone—at the price of bleeding fingertips—so that it fell into my cell. A small hole was left behind, through which I could observe liberty.

Elated, I immediately began to work upon an adjacent stone, and had the satisfaction—notwithstanding considerable more finger pain—of tumbling a second stone. Convinced I could make an even bigger hole, one that would allow me to wiggle out, I saw freedom within reach.

By that time, it must have been late afternoon. Though famished and thirsty, I worked hard upon the next stone until I heard footfalls beyond the prison door.

People were coming.

I leaped to shove the tumbled stones back into place and then flung some of the rotten hay over the debris I had made. I poked the leash knob back into the wall, where, to my relief, it stayed.

The door opened, and Mr. Sandys was there. This time, however, another man was with him, a scrawny, pot-bellied man of but modest height. With his thin fuzz of grizzled gray hair, something like the balls of dust that gather in corners, I took him to be old, 'tween fifty and sixty years of age. He also carried a strong stench of rum, sweat, and general uncleanliness. In short, at first sight, he was a most ill-favored fellow.

"Well, boy," exclaimed Mr. Sandys. "Here is a gentleman who will consider buying you."

CHAPTER TWENTY-THREE

In Which Mr. Sandys Does Me a Questionable Favor.

This newcomer barely entered the room, when he paused, peered about, and put a dirty hand to the knife stuck in his belt. It was as if he feared an attack, or perhaps it was he who would attack, because there was a pistol in his belt as well. Nor did he relax when he must have seen it was only me in the jail, but kept his hand on his weapon.

His face was unclean and ill shaved, with a small, round, and altogether purplish nose. His chin was hardly there, his flabby neck much like a turkey's wattle. As for his half-lidded and bleary eyes, they appraised me as if I were something contemptible, as suggested by the curl of disgust that showed upon his thin lips.

As for clothing, his shirt was stained, his waistcoat

filthy. In one dirty hand, he held a battered black hat. Scruffy leather boots shod his feet. He appeared to have no fashion at all, save being sloberly.

If I had come upon this man on the street, observing no hint of good manners, I would have given him good distance. Once past him, which I would have done in haste, I would have looked back to make sure he was not pursuing me.

To my eyes he was an altogether disgraceful fellow. Moreover, the impression of violence he projected caused me to immediately step back.

Yet—I thought—here was a man who might buy me and take me from the jail. Was he the best that Mr. Sandys or Annapolis could do? I hastened to remind myself that just because the man looked distasteful did not prove he was. As the saying goes: "A rough shirt can cover a silken heart."

With no salutation, the man curtly asked me some of the same questions the buyers on the ship had asked: my name, age, and crime, and the length of my sentence.

As I answered, I offered my best smile and stood in what I thought was a self-effacing posture.

The man made no response, but proceeded to do a rough jabbing and prodding of my arms and chest. All the while, he continued to study me with his bloodshot eyes as if to observe my value, if any.

At the end of his scrutiny, he turned to Mr. Sandys and said, "I'll give a five-pound tobacco note for him."

Mr. Sandys said, "I told you, sir: He's worth a hundred. You heard him, he can read and write."

The man grunted. "He'll have no need of such with me. No, I won't give more than five pounds."

Mr. Sandys considered me as if debating the point. Belatedly, I realized he was allowing me to make the decision.

Here was a hinge upon which the door of my life might well swing. Did I allow myself to be taken up by this repulsive man, or hope that someone superior might come along? But what if no one else wanted me? Yes, I had made progress in making a hole in the jail wall. Would it not be better to free myself? As it is said, a man beholden to someone for his freedom is not entirely free.

But while I'd made a small gap in the wall, I'd failed to divest myself from the leash, which was still attached to the iron ring round my neck. Anyone who saw me would know I was an escaped felon.

But I also told myself that going with this man would at least get me out of jail. Deciding between now or maybe never, I gave a small nod to Mr. Sandys. But please mind, I gave it tepidly.

"He's yours," pronounced Mr. Sandys, with a clear meaning of the deal is done. "Five pounds tobacco."

I had been sold.

Let me confess: I felt deep shamefulness that I was a party to this transaction, the selling of myself. Among other humiliations, I was sold cheaper than any of my fellow felons. I tried to console myself by thinking I'd advanced my situation: better out of jail than in.

All the same, there was a loud alarm bell tolling in my thoughts: Had I just committed another of my follies?

CHAPTER TWENTY-FOUR

My New Master Takes Possession of Me.

M r. Sandys took a rumpled paper from a pocket as well as a stump of charcoal. I presumed the paper transferred my ownership from the town of Annapolis to this off-putting man.

Sure enough, the man used the charcoal to mark the paper, something that looked like an *X*, which meant I was unable to learn his name. All the same, the signing meant I was now owned by this ill-natured character. Moreover, it was my decision, which made it happen. Let it be learned, a small nod can make a great shift.

By way of proof, Mr. Sandys released my leash from the wall and handed the loose end to this man, saying, "He belongs to you now.

"I wish you well, boy," Mr. Sandys said to me in an official-sounding voice. "But I'm obliged to warn you that insofar as I am the town's watchman, if I ever see you again without written permission from him"—a head cock toward my new owner—"I shall arrest you straightaway and things shall go badly for you."

To this formal warning, Mr. Sandys, in a more natural, friendly voice, added to me, "I pray we meet again in better circumstances." He went on to oblige me with a sardonic bow, adding an impish wink, meant to acknowledge his self-satisfaction in doing me a favor, even when he probably hadn't.

Then Mr. Sandys left—presumably to his watchman duties—leaving the cell door open. I supposed I'd never see this curious friend anymore. Which meant, once again, I felt abandoned.

My new master clapped his dirty hat upon his head, muttered something I didn't understand, and gave my leash a yank. I had no choice but to follow. At least, I told myself, I am out of jail. I cannot say I felt much elation.

The man walked on with a slow, somewhat ungainly stride. Perhaps it was from drink. Or his age. Not once did he look round at me or acknowledge my presence. Fully forlorn, I trudged along, anxious as to what might happen next.

We passed people twice, but he said naught to them, only glaring at them, hand to knife. One of the persons even moved out of my new master's way, whether out of fear or repugnance I could only guess.

I beg you to consider: There I was, in a whole new world, knowing nothing of my future. I had the sparsest knowledge of my owner, not so much as his name. He said nothing about where he lived, what use he would make of me, his trade or occupation. Did he live near or far? In town or out? In what kind of dwelling? Was there a kindly wife? Were there friendly children? Other servants I might befriend?

Yes, I was out of jail, but only to pass into a new, unknown world. Let me assure you, suspense about all these vital questions may be the spring that moves a story ticking forward like a fine clock. But to live a life in such a continually unexpected fashion is wearisome beyond belief.

Trust me, all ye who seek adventure: better a horizontal life than one that leaps from one high crisis to another.

CHAPTER TWENTY-FIVE

Which Contains Alarming
Information about My Master.

My owner led me to a nearby tavern called the Royal George, a one-story, wooden structure on the northern edge of town. Its outside walls were planked much like the hull of a ship, and of a reddish hue. Two windows. Shutters. A chimney at one end.

We entered—me in tow—the man pausing at the threshold to look within, as if to determine who was there. Just as when he entered the jail, he put his hand to his knife.

He seemed to distrust everyone and everything.

The establishment we entered consisted of one room with a brick floor. Wooden pillars stood in the corners. To one side was a stone fireplace, a small fire ablaze, which soothed the evening's edge of chill. A lit lamp was attached to one wall, which along with some bees-wax candles on two of the tables diminished the room's dullness.

On the far wall was an enclosed area, behind which a small, gray-haired man was dispensing drinks. The smells of rum, cider, and tobacco fumed the air. Mind, it was nothing such as I experienced in London taverns, which were close, crowded, and clamorous. This was a little lake of lazy leisure.

There were three round tables—no room for more—at which six men were sitting, talking, and drinking, two of them smoking clay pipes. When we entered, one of the men at a table called out, "Mr. Fitzhugh, sir. Good day to you."

My owner's reply to such civilities was little more than a throaty grunt. In any case I learned his name. Fitzhugh.

"Got yourself a new servant?" asked another.

"Aye," he said.

"What happened to the other?"

Fitzhugh pulled his pistol from his belt and pointed it into the air. "Dead," he said.

Shocked, I took his meaning to be dead by his hand. On the instant my stomach turned queasy.

One of the men seemed to agree with me. He said, "God have mercy. How?"

"He was about to run off," was Fitzhugh's sneered

reply. "You know the law. I'd have to pay two hundred pounds of tobacco if someone else caught him, wouldn't I? Got rid of him myself and bought a cheaper replacement." Using his pistol, he gestured toward me.

"And the one who ran, did you have to track him far?"

"Never got off my land." Fitzhugh spoke with a bully's bravado, as if what he'd said was something altogether common, with him at least.

"Good," said another man. "They need to learn the lesson. It helps to keep the others down."

Who, I wondered, were the others that needed such a lesson? Was life and death all so casual here?

I had been uneasy about my new master. Now I was deeply alarmed.

Mr. Fitzhugh led me to a corner of the room. There, as if giving a command to a dog, he ordered me to sit and pointed to the floor. When I complied, he tied my leash— also doglike—to one of the wooden pillars. Then he went to the sole unoccupied table and sat down in a chair with as much grace as a frog settles himself into mud.

Full of disquiet, I kept my eyes on him. Fitzhugh did not engage in conversation with any of the other men. All the same, he stole distrustful glances at them, as if wanting to alert himself for sudden attacks.

Given the harsh way he had dealt with me, displayed

his gun, spoke and acted toward the tavern customers, I was now convinced he was a man of frothing anger.

Dear Lord, I thought, I should never have allowed myself to be bought by this man. Oliver, I added, you have committed yet another gross folly.

This self-reproach was followed by the self-warning: But willy-nilly, you are owned by him. Be watchful.

A young woman approached him. At first glance she appeared to be the same age as Charity, about eighteen. Indeed, for a heart-stopping moment, I thought the lass might be my sister. Of course, I was wrong.

Fitzhugh spoke gruffly to her.

She went off and came back with a full pewter tankard. It smelled like rum. When she came up behind Mr. Fitzhugh and tapped him on the shoulder, he sprang up and around, his knife instantly in hand. Much frightened, she jumped back, so that the drink sloshed on the floor.

"Stupid girl," Fitzhugh roared. "Don't come on me like that. Get another."

The other patrons were equally startled.

The servant girl, jaw clenched, face pale, wiped the liquid from the floor with her apron then scooted off and returned, this time cautiously approaching the old man from the front.

He snatched the tankard, gave no thanks, but drank, and continued to do so, adrenching himself, as it were, in his liquor. As I watched, I added another trait to his character: I was tethered, nay, owned, by a sodden, dead-hearted person.

CHAPTER TWENTY-SIX

What the Servant Girl Told Me.

As time passed, Fitzhugh continued to drink, though now and again he glanced at me, wanting to make sure, it seemed, that I remained where he'd put me. I worked to keep my face blank.

Some of the other men left the tavern, others entered, but Fitzhugh no more engaged with the new ones— except for quick nods—than with those who had been there before. The old man was clearly known, and just as clearly avoided. My disgust grew apace.

After a while, Fitzhugh tipped his filthy slouch hat forward, laid his arms down on the table, lowered his head, and, to all appearances, fell asleep. His noisome breathing consisted of grunts and clogged throat clearings.

As the old man continued to sleep, I considered unfastening my leash from round the wooden pillar and bolting, but feared what the other men in the tavern would do. Might they not want to teach me a gross lesson?

Or what might happen if Fitzhugh woke and discovered me in flight? Would he shoot me? The truth is, though acquainted with him for but a short time, I already feared him.

I therefore stayed where I was, full of unease, while Fitzhugh slept on, until the servant girl approached me.

"Boy," she said in a whispered voice. "Are you hungry?"

I offered up a smile. "Yes, please," I said. "And thirsty. But I have no money."

She glanced at Fitzhugh, with some fear. "I have some old bread," she said, and went off.

I did muse if I would ever eat anything besides bread.

Within moments, she returned with a coarse loaf and a pewter cup of apple cider. I took both with fulsome—if quiet—thanks, gulping the cider and devouring the bread as fast as possible, lest my master rebuke me.

She stole a quick, watchful glance at Fitzhugh and then said, "Why are you with him?" Her voice was low.

"Do you know him?" I asked.

"Enough to know I don't wish to know him more."

"Why? What is he?"

Another quick look. More whispering. "He's a vicious, offending man. He trusts no one, affronts all."

"Why?"

"He thinks the whole world wishes to steal from him."

"Has he anything to steal?"

"It's said he has only a little and is much given to drink. You're wearing the iron collar. Does he own you?"

Here I was confronted with a problem I'd failed to consider: How—now that I was asked directly—was I to describe my condition? I hesitated, fearful that the plight of a transported felon might repel the girl. The truth is, I had as deep a hunger for kindliness as food.

Before I could speak, she, in a forgiving voice, told me, "You need say no more."

Her sympathy moved me to blurt out—albeit in a whisper—"Please, mistress, I'm a transported felon, just arrived. Fitzhugh bought me for my seven years of labor."

The look of sympathy on her face was sweet, but equally alarming.

"How old are you?" she said in a gentle voice.

"Twelve."

She sighed, gazed at my iron collar, and then, with a face full of pity, whispered, "Be warned. Mr. Fitzhugh is a violent man."

"Please, miss," I said in haste, "I have a sister. Older than me. She was also transported. She looks somewhat like you. Her name is Charity. Charity Pitts. I need to find her." I held up the lace bit. "Have you heard the name spoken?"

She shook her head. "But you have my miseration, boy, and I wish you God's good blessing."

I thought of asking her to untie me but too late, she hastened away.

Though touched by this young woman's compassion, I could only be further distressed by her words about Fitzhugh. Everything was foretelling that I would be in great need of kindness. But where I might find it, I had no idea. As for her knowing nothing of Charity, it was, alas, only what I expected.

Since my new master remained asleep I had little choice but to stay in place. Yet the girl's words about my master, plus my own observation as to his ferocity, his drinking, and that he had appeared to have murdered his previous servant, convinced me that escape was urgent.

CHAPTER TWENTY-SEVEN

In Which I Spend My First Night
in the New World.

Given what the serving girl said, I thought she might help me flee, but before she returned, Fitzhugh woke. Without warning, he sat up and looked about, his small nose a deeper shade of purple than before, his cheeks ruddy, his face collapsed. For a moment, he affixed his dull eyes on me as if it were a struggle for him to recall who I was. Indeed, he continued to stare, rub his face with the heel of his hand, and chew his lower lip as if in a quandary.

I waited anxiously. What was he about to do?

At last, he stood, made his wobbly way to the tapster, and marked his bill. Then he untied my leash from the pillar, gave it a pull, and led me outside. The fact that it had grown completely dark seemed to confound him. Still, no words were exchanged. He tugged my leash and led me behind the tavern. There was an open stable where a big brown horse was tied near a box of grass. Mr. Fitzhugh approached the horse and patted his neck, and muttered some words into his ear, which suggested the horse belonged to him. In all this time I had been with him, we'd had nothing that might have been called a conversation. As far as I was aware he didn't know my name.

At least he talked to his horse.

My master gathered up some grass from the box and dumped it on the ground. Then he turned to me and abruptly pushed me down. "Hands together," he commanded.

Having no choice, I did as bid, at which point he bound my hands and feet. He also attached my leash to a wall—out of reach.

That done, he lay down, scooped more grass to form a kind of pillow for himself, put his dirty hat over his eyes, and went back to his sodden, noisy sleep.

Given the opportunity, I grappled with my bindings, trying to pull my hands and feet free, but it proved impossible. I could not even stand. In the end, I had little choice but to try to make myself comfortable by propping my back against a wall.

As I remained there, altogether miserable, have no doubts; all my thoughts were given over to the notion that I must set myself free as soon as possible. How mind-numbing the thought. How many times had I struggled to free myself?

Yet the painful, mournful reality was, all my efforts had failed.

CHAPTER TWENTY-EIGHT

In Which I Put My Reading Skills to Use.

It was early next morning, still chilly, when Fitzhugh woke me with a hard foot to my ribs. I had slept ill and was stiff and sore. Though Fitzhugh untied my numb hands and feet, I needed help to stand, which he gave but roughly.

"All right now, boy," he demanded as he hauled me to my feet, "what's your name?"

My hands prickly with pain, I stood there and replied, "Oliver Cromwell Pitts."

"Oliver will do." He tapped my chest with a hard-nailed finger. "Call me Master."

How repulsive the term. But what choice did I have? "Yes, Master," I said.

"Do as you're told, and we'll get on. Otherwise . . ." He put hands to pistol and blade and let the unspoken threat hover before me. Clearly, he liked to menace people. I was afraid to reply.

Then he announced, "I need food."

He untied his horse and led it and me—both on leads—to the front of the tavern, where there was early daylight. There he came up close and said, "Just know, by Maryland law for each day you run off, ten days will be added to your term of labor. Be gone a month and I'll add a year."

What else could I do but nod?

With that he left me to go back into the tavern.

Being unattended, it came to mind that I should mount the horse and gallop off. You will recall, I hope, that Captain Hawkes (in England) had taught me to ride.

Alas, I had no idea where to go, and was cowed by Fitzhugh's threats and what he had said about the local law. No doubt, the iron collar round my neck would reveal me for what I was, a felon. Just as the serving girl had noticed it, surely others, not so kind, would too. It was one thing to hide in a swarming London. Annapolis appeared an impossible place to keep out of sight.

As I stood there, I noticed a board affixed to one side of the tavern door, upon which many bills were posted.

Ran away, A servant girl, named Susanna. Said Susanna is a slender Negro of middle stature, very dark eyebrows, blind in left eye. She is a skilled spinner. Escaped from the Subscriber, in Maryland on Potowmack River. Amos Dalton.

In search of my husband, Edward Sitrow, printer, aged Sixty-six, who ran off with a servant wench by the name of Belinda Wright. Please inform Mistress Abby Thacher at the Sign of the Bell, Philadelphia. Reward. Mary Sitrow.

Run away from Mr. Thomas Bonny: Charles, a white indentured servant, a cooper by trade he is of a middle size and about 40 years, speaks an elegant English, and is a crafty fellow, supposed to have fled to St. Mary's, Maryland. Any person who takes him up shall have five pounds reward in cash or tobacco.

Ran away, a new black from Africa named Cuffee aged about 23, of very dark complexion, short but well set, and very sullen. He is supposed to make for Annapolis. Reward. Alexander Mothwick.

There were more announcements, just as arresting. I tried to recall if I had seen such postings in England.

Perhaps I had never noticed them. Regardless, here was proof that in this world many were running away, a disturbing judgment on the place. But if these people had gone off and, as these postings suggested, were successful in freeing themselves, so might I.

Then it occurred to me there might be a notice about Charity.

But before I could read more, Fitzhugh returned. In his dirty hand was yet another old piece of bread, which he tore in parts, keeping two-thirds for himself, giving me the rest. He also carried a heavy stink of new rum.

He must have observed that I had been looking at the notifications, for he said, "Can you read?" It made it sound like an accusation.

Realizing he had forgotten that he'd previously asked me the question, I made an instant change. "No, sir. Not at all."

He gave a grunt, nodded to the papers, and then waved a hand at the postings. "Servants try to run away, but no one gets far. Do you know why?"

I shook my head.

"When someone like you bolts off, I gain many friends. We all do. We hunt runaways down; catch them and the worse for them. They say"—he gestured toward the notices—"they want their freedom. All they get is an early grave."

Recalling his conversation of the day before, I took the warning as reality and said nothing.

Nonetheless, he put his hand to his pistol. "Run off and I'll shoot you," he announced with just that curtness. Then he added, "I'm a fair shot."

"Yes, sir," I replied, not wishing to debate the point.

His bragging demanded more. He pulled the pistol from his belt, cocked the flint, took a one-eyed aim at the hitching post, and pulled the trigger. There was a spurt of flame, a loud report. The top of the post shattered.

If he had desired to terrify me, he succeeded. Moreover, he had also informed me that he kept his pistol loaded, primed, and ready to use.

The old man fixed my leash to his saddle, swung himself upon his horse, and started off. Since I was still attached to the lead, I was obliged to follow at his pace, not quite a run, not quite a walk, rather a jog-trot, which soon proved fatiguing.

I looked back. People—including the servant girl— had come out of the tavern to see why the gun went off. How I wished I could have run back and begged for help. Alas, I was being pulled away. Of course, I had no idea where we were going. Nor did I—all too aware how my master could use his pistol—dare to take as much as one step toward freedom. All I knew was that with every stride I took, I was being led by a truly dreadful man toward what I assumed would be an equally dreadful life.

CHAPTER TWENTY-NINE

In Which I Journey to My New Home.

Annapolis being a small town, we soon left it behind and traveled along a well-used track, which I thought led us northerly. I never paused because if I slowed I was summarily jolted along. Once I did stumble and fall, only to be dragged some ways. It was not Mr. Fitzhugh who stopped, but the horse, which—perhaps feeling the weight—halted long enough for me to regain my feet and start anew. Full of anguish and exhaustion, a bleeding, scuffed shoulder, my breath a mixture of gasps and sobs, my sides aching, I went on, following after Fitzhugh.

The way was thickly bordered by tall trees, of kinds unknown to me save oak. Birds were abundant. Now and again I caught glimpses of water. Perhaps it was the Severn River or the Chesapeake Bay, though it might have been some other watercourse or inlet. As I hurried along, I worked hard to remember our way, in hopes I might gain the opportunity to flee back to Annapolis.

You may be sure I had no plan as to what I would do in Annapolis. It was simply that the English ships at the quay seemed closer to the world I knew, and thus drew me, even as I was pulled the other way. I also recalled the kindness of the tavern girl. Nothing attracts more than hints of heart.

Now and again we met people coming toward town— men and women both—but no words, only brief gestures were exchanged between Fitzhugh and others. People seemed to know him, and accordingly edged away. Yet, if I had understood him correctly, they would willingly join him to pursue me if I ran for freedom.

People did look at me—tethered as I was—with what I took to be a mix of bafflement and alarm, but no rebuke was sent to Fitzhugh.

I wanted to cry out, "Help me," but was fearful as to what my owner might do.

Some of the people we passed were Negroes, but I was unable to determine if they were enslaved or not. I presumed so. One did have an iron collar much like mine. What impressed me was that they were unattended by white people, giving the illusion that they were free (and some perhaps were) but I was convinced most were bound by invisible chains. Indeed, I recalled that someone on the *Owners Goodwill* told me that all of British America had slaves.

We went on then, ceaselessly, me on my leash, sharing no words, struggling to keep up, with no idea where we were going or how far.

At some point, we made a turn and came upon a river's edge. The wide waterway was flowing swiftly, so that it coiled with white water. Tied to a planked wharf was a raft-like boat, upon which a man sat smoking a pipe. He was great chested, with arms like tree trunks and a fierce beard fringing his face. He made me think of a wild beast.

From one side of the river to the other, a rope had been strung, the rope attached to poles on opposite riverbanks. On the far side was a little house. Perhaps the man lived there.

Fitzhugh dismounted and led his horse down a slight embankment. With me following we stepped upon this odd craft.

The man on it stood. "Mr. Fitzhugh, sir."

"Mr. Eps," was the brief return.

Nothing more.

As soon as Fitzhugh, the horse, and I stood in the middle of the flatboat, this Mr. Eps grasped the rope that stretched across the river and began to haul on it with his huge hands. Thus we moved across the river in short jerks. I soon grasped the reason for his muscles since the flow of the river, stronger than I imagined, kept pushing the bow of the boat around as we slowly moved across.

On my part, I tried to gauge the river's depth. If I was fleeing, would I be able to wade across? It seemed unlikely. Which meant this river would be a major obstacle to my return to Annapolis. Recalling Moco Jack and his ability to swim, I reminded myself I must learn the art.

We soon reached the far shore, where Fitzhugh led his horse—and me—onto land again.

"I'll put the reckoning in my book," Mr. Eps called after us as we stepped off his boat.

Fitzhugh did no more than raise a hand. At least it wasn't his pistol.

We continued along, me moving as before, without rest, on a narrower trail, endless trees pressing in from either side. I sensed we were going deeper into what I could only call a wilderness, farther from the world I knew.

There was a sensation of new spring growth, that early bright season of green that fairly glows with newness. As for sounds, the chirp of birds, and now and again the rustle of leaves, was soothing. From time to time, on my right, I caught glimpses of broad, bright water, vast enough to make me think I was still going northward, parallel to the Chesapeake Bay.

I tried to tell myself it was all appealing, but tethered as I was, endlessly pulled along at a trot, body sore, and breath short, it was hard to feel it. How free and open it all seemed. How constricted was I.

At one point I was sure I heard an abrupt thrashing among the trees, as if someone or something was smashing through the forest. Startled, I stared hard and was sure I saw a dark, bulky creature, but whether human or beast I could not tell. Since Fitzhugh seemed neither to notice nor care, I could not stop. I hurried on a little faster, that I might be nearer to him. My hunger grew, too.

We passed no towns or settlements. But I did see people at work, mostly black folk, but there were other workers, white people. Perhaps they were felons like me, maybe indentured servants, all serving their time. Though the area was far more populated than I thought at first, all these places fronted the bay.

For a brief time, there was rain. I was bitten, too, by a cloud of tiny insects, which I kept trying to slap away.

"Mosquitoes," Fitzhugh called back over his shoulder.

We crossed many a small, rushing stream and low inlets, the water swollen. Spring freshets, I supposed. At one point, we had to pass over another wide river, another flatboat that required poling.

What I learned was that the way back to Annapolis—if I ever took it—would be long, hard, and wet.

At last the old man called out, "We're almost home."

That greatly relieved me, and as new circumstances

inevitably do, somewhat restored some strength and made me curious, but equally apprehensive. It is painful to come home to a place you never knew and did not want. Whereas the word "home" should mean comfort, here it only added to my deep disquiet.

CHAPTER THIRTY

In Which I View My New Home and Learn What It Was.

Not long after Fitzhugh spoke, we turned from the trail and moved out from beneath the trees. He came off his horse.

"This is mine," he proclaimed like some monarch reclaiming his kingdom.

Before us lay an open space, which sloped down until it reached a massive spread of water, which I supposed was the Chesapeake Bay.

Closer at hand were separate fields, but little—if anything—seemed to be growing in them. Some buildings of various sizes were clustered together below. All seemed in a state of neglect, with lap-sided planking askew, shingles curled like old leaves. If they were dwelling places or served some other function, I was unable to tell.

I also caught a glimpse of what might have been a warped wharf that poked into the bay.

What I would discover was that Fitzhugh owned—compared to others—a modest amount of property that he cultivated. He had owned it for about seven years, the previous owner having died. Fitzhugh called it his plantation, though it was barely enough to keep him alive and in drink.

As we continued on, I observed a Negro man in the fields. He had a hoe in his hands and was working. As Fitzhugh led me and his horse over the land, this person looked up briefly. I had no doubt the old man saw him, too, but no words of greeting were exchanged. But this, as I had already witnessed, was the old man's manner.

Fitzhugh first took me to the small stable where he tied up his horse. Next to it was a dirty enclosure where he had fenced in some hogs. There were three such creatures, huge, black-haired, dung-crusted, with upright ears and long, snuffling, drippy snouts. When I appeared, they lifted their massive heads and studied me with small, malevolent eyes, grunting all the while.

"You'll feed them." Fitzhugh pointed to a large wooden box, filled with corn cobs. "Put a hand by their faces and they'll bite it off." For once he actually grinned.

Next, he guided me to the smallest building on his land, being but one story. The outside walls had been made of horizontal, rough cut slabs of cypress wood, with what looked to be mud filling the gaps between the boards. Like the other structures, it was much in need of repair. If winters were severe I'd not like to be within.

Fitzhugh thrust open a narrow, low door, its old leather hinges making a soft creak. "Where I live," he announced. For the first time, he unfastened my leash (my iron collar remained) and shoved me roughly toward the entryway only to abruptly hold me back, saying, "You are never to go in unless I'm here."

"Yes, sir."

"And forbidden to go near the bay."

I merely nodded.

"Pay heed," he declared, pulling me around so my face was close to his face and noxious reek. "I only do what I want, when I want. If you try to stop me, I'll kill you. Understood?"

"Yes, sir."

"Then enter."

I stepped within the house and was immediately struck by the fusty smell of old food, sweat, and dirt. In such little light as there was I saw all that was to be seen. The whole building was barely twenty feet by twenty (rather like my recent prison) and had a dirt floor. The one small window had open shutters. Overhead were rough cut beams, upon which boards lay. Alongside one wall was a crude ladder going up, perhaps to a storage or sleeping place.

Against another wall was a jagged stone fireplace. A hook dangled from the flue and upon it hung an iron pot, used, I supposed, for cooking. Partly charred logs lay below in an overflowing ash heap. In front of the hearth, which would be the warmest place, was a low, narrow platform that might have been a bed.

On the same wall, to one side, hung a musket and a powder horn. Also, a basket of what looked like onions. Another basket of what I soon learned was Indian corn. A bag of beans. Filches of some kind of dried meat hung from other hooks. They gave off the smell of rot.

In the room's center was a trestle table, with half-hewn logs on rods, which served—I supposed—as a sitting place. On the table sat a candle-holder and dirty wooden trenchers, on which lay remnants of food and bones.

A closed chest, also made of wood, sat on the floor a few feet from the table. Some items of dirty clothing hung carelessly on pegs that poked out from the walls.

All in all, it was rude, filthy, without much comfort. Indeed, a miserable place. A momentary memory of my English home engulfed me. How different this Maryland was in every way from that, how remote a country I'd come to, how far removed I was from what was my home, what I chose to call true society. Yet I was to remain here—such was my sentence—for seven years.

How could I not think then of my life—my carefree life—with my beloved sister, Charity, and with my sometimes difficult father, in England? As I stood there I was sure I had come to the end of the world. My heart was filled with grief.

"You will sleep up there," Fitzhugh said, pointing toward the ceiling. "Along with Bara. If you try to come down and out, you'll have to get by me. I won't let you."

"Please, sir, who is Bara?"

"My slave."

I assumed that was who I'd seen on the way in. "Is there anyone else, sir?"

"Don't want any women to pester me. And I have no children. Be just us three.

"To the east is the bay, fifteen miles across, Kent Island. You swim?"

"No, sir."

"Good. Annapolis is south. Plenty of people from here to there, but your iron collar will tell folks what you are. Go without permission and you'll be taken. When you're caught, things will go badly. I'll see to that.

"To the west is a swamp that goes on for more miles than I know.

"Six miles north is another wide, deep river. Have I made myself clear? There's no way to get away from here.

"We three will either get along or not." He pointed across the room to the musket hanging on the wall.

To all this he added, "You'll remain for seven years. When your time is up, I'll set you free. Consider yourself lucky: Bara will never go."

I confess, though I thought I had no tears left within, at his words my eyes welled up and I struggled to blink my emotion away. Seven years . . .

He asked, "Anything to say to that?"

No doubt because I felt desperate, into my head came the words my messmate Rufus Caulwell told me about a swamp, that it was a way to get back to England. Perhaps it was this swamp to which he was referring. Thinking, however, it would be best to show ignorance, I said, "What is a . . . swamp?"

"Gross wetlands," he returned. "Impossible to get through. Disgusting blood water, which you'd be an idiot to drink, along with muck that will swallow you whole. If the mosquitoes don't eat you, the snakes, bears, or lions will. If you see a beast, you're already too close."

I stared at him. Was there no end to horrors?

"Now, you need to meet Bara. I'll say it once: Make sure you get along with him. That's why I bought you."

Someone else to fear, then.

We walked out. A hoe was leaning against the house. Fitzhugh snatched it up and tossed it to me. "Follow me. It's time for you to get to work."

CHAPTER THIRTY-ONE

In Which I Meet Bara.

Fitzhugh led me up an incline, across open fields, heading near the stand of trees where I had seen this Bara working.

"It's planting time," he said. "We're going to a seedbed."

Being ignorant of what he was talking about, and exceedingly on edge, I said nothing. Indeed, I walked as slowly as I dared, not wishing to meet another objectionable person. I would have given much to be alone.

We came under some trees, where a large square area had been cleared. The soil there was covered by what looked to be a layer of gray ash. Squatting on his haunches, his back to us, I presumed, was Bara.

"Bara," Mr. Fitzhugh cried out. "Here's Oliver. In place of Clark."

The man stood up, turned and faced me. Immediately

I saw that he was not a man, but a boy only somewhat older than me.

I had witnessed some black people in England who were either laborers or servants. There were never that many, nothing such as I had already observed in Maryland, from the quay through the streets of Annapolis. And in England, whether these black people were slaves or not, I readily confess I never knew and never asked. Let my excuse be I had never been so near to a black person as I was now. As I looked upon this boy with a mix of unease and curiosity, my only concern was how he would treat me, following Fitzhugh's command that we get along.

Bara was taller than me, so that I had to look up. His neck was somewhat long, his shoulders broad, arms bare, sinewy, tight with muscle. His clothing was rough: old trousers and a sleeveless jacket, both articles made of cheap linen.

His hands were large, with long fingers. His narrow feet were bare. His hair was black, thick, and tightly curled. As for his face, which was almost ebony, it was thin, almost gaunt, his nose small. His mouth, thin lipped, neither smiled nor frowned—indeed showed no emotion—as he studied me intently.

I also observed how still he was. Indeed, as I would come to know, Bara had a way of standing self-contained, almost as if he were breathing, though of course he was.

It was as if most of what he was, was within, and he had little desire of letting anything out.

When he first considered me I perceived no feeling, but his eyes took command. His look seemed to survey, evaluate, and appraise me yet no word was spoken.

"Teach him," said Fitzhugh to Bara. "He needs to get to work." With no further words, the old man left.

CHAPTER THIRTY-TWO

My First Time with Bara.

For some time, we two boys stood in silence, each of us trying to appraise the other.

"What's your name?" Bara finally asked in a voice that told me no more than his expression, though his English was much like mine.

"Oliver."

"He own you?"

I nodded.

"Indentured?"

"Transported convict."

He cocked his head slightly to one side and waited for me to say more.

"I was convicted of a crime," I admitted. "In England."

"A thief," he said, though there was no judgment in his tone. "What crime did you do?"

"Stole money."

"How much?"

"Twenty-three shillings. I was transported here. Mr. Fitzhugh bought me. I'm to stay seven years."

"'Oliver' your real name, or one he gave you?"

"My own. Did he give you your name?"

"My parents gave it to me. From Guinea, but I don't remember them. How old are you?"

"Twelve."

"Young thief."

"Why are you here?" I ventured.

"Fitzhugh's slave."

"How old are you?"

"More than you, I'd guess. But not by much." He turned to look at the ash on the ground. "You know anything about growing tobacco?"

I shook my head.

"Nothing?"

"Nothing."

"I suppose then I have to teach you everything."

I could only nod and wait for instruction.

He studied me for yet another while. "You mind that it's me that will have to learn you?"

"Should I?" My voice trembled.

"Me being black. A slave. You being white."

I could not hold back. "I don't know anything about

147

tobacco," I said, my voice suddenly breaking. "I don't know where we are. Or about Fitzhugh. Or where I am. Or you. I don't know anything." As tears coursed down my cheek, I stood there ashamed, my head bowed. Given the choice I would have just as soon died then and there.

Bara only said, "Tears won't get you much."

I wanted to say, "I just need a friend," but could not find the words, and besides, I was fearful this Bara would rebuff or mock me.

When I finally forced myself to look up, he was still observing me. "You're right then," he said. "You know nothing." Again, it was not a judgment. It was a fact. As for friendship, he said naught.

Feeling powerless, but wanting to say something, I said, "Who was Clark?" giving the name of the person I heard Fitzhugh say I was replacing.

"A boy like me. Maybe younger. Slave."

"What happened to him?"

Bara lifted his shoulders and let them drop. "The old man killed him. He's like that. Any idea why you're here?"

"To labor."

Bara said, "You're Clark's replacement. He was all right. About your age. I liked him well enough. But he didn't think. A noddy. He let slip he was going to run away. Fitzhugh acted first."

"I heard Fitzhugh brag he killed someone," I said.

"Clark, probably."

"Did you see him do it?"

"Didn't have to. Clark just disappeared."

I stared at Bara. He went on: "So if you think about running away, better keep your thoughts silent or you'll replace Clark in another way."

Bara said it just like that. Bluntly. But knowing I was the replacement for that murdered boy made me feel ill.

Bara said, "So I guess the first learning I can give you is: Don't ever talk back to the old man. Just listen. Do what he asks. Make sure you know that. Another thing, he's quick to malice and you'll never know why. Violent. Drunk. No friends I ever noticed. If he has mercy, I've never seen it. He's got a horse and hogs and cares more for them than us. We're just his tools, his servants, nothing more."

Bara considered me for yet another long while, as if trying to make up his mind what else to say or do. Then he bent down, to reach into a small leather bag that lay by his feet. He brought something out and opened his hand before me. In his palm lay powdery brown specks.

"What's that?" I asked.

"Tobacco seeds. This is planting time. It's the way we start. Around here, that's the way everything begins."

"When does it end?"

"Never," he said, and that one small word settled upon me like a thousand pounds of weight.

CHAPTER THIRTY-THREE

A Brief Digression about Tobacco.

To fathom the world into which I had come, you must learn—as I had to—about tobacco, the word given into English by the island people of Haiti.

In our ancient English language, to be a "sot" meant one was a dolt, a blockhead, a stupid person. So it was that "sot-weed" was a common term for tobacco. Which is to say, some people believed that smoking tobacco turned you into a "sot," or the smoking thereof is something that sots did.

My father, who drank far too much and suffered much for it, loathed tobacco. No friend of English kings, he oft quoted King James the First's remark that tobacco was "a custom loathsome to the eye, hateful to the nose, harmful to the brain, dangerous to the lungs, and in the black stinking fume thereof, nearest resembles the horrible smoke of the pit that is Hell."

England, and Europe, however, had gone mass mad for tobacco. Thus, in the new world, tobacco was king. More than king: It was everything. The entire Chesapeake Bay area was called the "Tobacco Coast," because it was so given over to the cultivation of that weed. It was the economy. Indeed, as you might recall from my account of the convict sale, tobacco itself was often used as money.

To grow it, care for it, harvest it, and send it on to England and Europe is a process that extends from spring to late fall. Bara and I worked at it every day from early light to early shadows, often in the summer's greatest heat. Endless hours with a hoe for weeding of the big green-leafed plant that grew as high as seven feet. Constant picking off damaging bugs, working among plants with fumes so noxious that being midst them sometimes made me ill and dizzy.

There followed cutting, staking, and drying until the time came for packing the leaves into barrel-like containers called hogsheads—four feet high, two and a half feet in diameter, weighing more than a thousand pounds when full—which were used for shipping.

A sloop would come up the Chesapeake, tie up at Fitzhugh's wharf—and countless other wharfs along the bay—collect the tobacco hogsheads to bring back to Annapolis, where it was graded, sold, and sent on to England and Europe.

The point is, tobacco was the chief and sometimes only cultivated crop, often the sole source of income, the primary foundation of wealth by the bay. For Fitzhugh, it was the sole means by which he lived and came to own me.

To put it precisely, I had become a sot-weed slave.

CHAPTER THIRTY-FOUR

How I Survived My First Day of Labor.

Following Bara's instructions, I worked the hoe for the rest of that day. I broke the earth, made rows, placed tiny seeds in the ground. Bara was firm in his directions, finding fault to be sure, but never harsh. For that I was grateful and did the best I could. We hardly talked, and when we did it was confined to work. It was clear: He was in charge. I tried not to think, just worked. Now and again I wiped tears away, but if Bara observed this, he said nothing.

His silence became my silence.

I have no idea how long we labored, enough to make me long for the work to end. Recall that my day had begun in Annapolis, at dawn, so the hours were long. Save for a bit of bread, I had eaten nothing. We stopped work only when the shadows of the trees crossed our working space.

"Time enough," Bara announced.

I felt much relief.

Then he and I walked back—me following—to Fitzhugh's house. As we went along he said, "Don't talk to me in the house. He thinks everyone is after him."

"Are they?" I ventured.

"Should be."

Before we went into the house, Bara led me into the hog pen. The great hogs, clearly knowing him, gathered round, grunting and snuffling. From a large wooden box, Bara gathered up an armful of corn ears and dropped them onto the ground. The hogs began to eat loudly.

I said, "Fitzhugh told me they were hurtful."

"They bite. But one of our jobs," he said.

We entered the dim house. Fitzhugh was at the table, working on a leather harness by the light of a single candle. A few metal tools lay nearby. As we came in, Fitzhugh looked up at Bara. "Will he do?"

"Will."

The old man reached down and lifted an earthenware jug to his mouth and drank. It smelled like rum. Then he made a flicking motion toward the hearth. It seemed to be a signal because Bara went to it. With a long-handled wooden spoon, he scooped out some yellow stuff from the iron pot and plopped it into three wooden bowls.

Fitzhugh watched as if appraising how much was ladled.

Bara handed a bowl to Fitzhugh, one to me, and kept one. The old man had the most. Then Bara went to one of the walls and sat down against it. I joined him.

We had been given no spoons, so using his fingers, Bara began to scoop up what was in the bowl and eat. Now and again he licked his fingers.

I stared into the bowl, wondering what I had been offered. Food, yes. But what? A yellow mush. Beans. Some chunks of meat. All mixed together. I looked to Bara.

Low voiced, he said, "Hog meat and hoecake."

"Hoecake?"

"Corn."

"No talking," shouted Fitzhugh.

Following Bara's example, I scooped some out and began to eat. It was gritty and bland, with only remnants of meat to chew. But it was food and I was glad to have it. Noticing that Bara ate slowly, I did the same.

When we finished eating—all too soon—Bara and I remained sitting. I was still hungry and licked my fingers. Now and again I glanced at Bara, trying to guess what to do. Bara stared straight ahead. He didn't speak, so I didn't either.

Fitzhugh continued to work, bent over his table like some foul troll. Now and again he'd pause and, frowning, peer at us, as if to make sure we remained in place. I think I heard him mumble to himself. Outside, it was completely dark, the cabin that much dimmer. I struggled to keep my eyes open.

At length, Fitzhugh completed his work. He shut the door—fixed it with a latch—and shuttered the window.

From the wall, he took down the musket and placed it by what I had supposed was a bed. He kept the pistol in his hand, blew out the candle, and lay down. In all this no words were spoken.

Save for the moonlight that leaked through gaps in the shutters, the cabin was dark.

As if Fitzhugh's actions were a signal, Bara stood up, prodded me on the shoulder, and went toward the ladder. Climbing, he paused once and looked at me. I took his meaning and followed slowly.

We crawled into a dark space, a close, bare attic loft. Some moonlight was visible in the cracks of the loft walls. By then, my eyes had grown accustomed to such light as there was.

Bara drew near and whispered, "Be careful. He'll be testing you."

"How?"

"You'll see."

"Please, can we talk?"

"No. He'll be listening."

He lay down on the wooden planking some distance from me. I also got down, my bones aching.

Within moments I heard Bara's sleeping breath.

I was exhausted, yet I could not sleep. The floor was bumpy. I was cold. From below I heard mutters and rumbles, and now and again a snore.

I reached into my pocket. In panic, I could not find that bit of Charity's lace. Then I touched it. I took it out, felt it, and even kissed it. "I will find you," I whispered to myself, and then replaced it.

The moon must have moved, so the darkness pressed on me, enveloping me like a suffocating cocoon. I told myself I had little choice but to endure. Then I recalled Bara's words about Fitzhugh: "He'll be testing you."

I tried to imagine what might happen but could not. I only knew I had no desire for tomorrow to come, but would have been content to sleep forever.

It was not to be so.

CHAPTER THIRTY-FIVE

In Which I Portray a Singular Kind of Life.

I must have slept, for Bara woke me at dawn and we went forth to work, hoes in hand. When Bara and I crawled down the ladder, the old man was still asleep— still snorting—on his pallet. Where infants might clutch a poppet, he had his pistol. As I would learn, Bara seemed to have a clock within that told him to get up before Fitzhugh; his way of avoidance.

Outside, the weather was gray and gloomy, with occasional spits of cold rain. It made me shiver.

Instead of going directly to the fields, Bara went to the stable, more of an open shed where the horse was kept. He took up an armful of what looked like dry grass from a big box and dropped it in front of the horse, which whinnied in appreciation and began to feed.

Next, he went to the hog pen. The hogs, seeing Bara, pushed about, grunting, clearly knowing he was there to feed them. This he did, hauling corn from a large box and throwing it on the ground. The hogs began to eat noisily.

"We going to get any food?" I inquired as we walked out to the fields for my first full day of work.

"What we ate last night," he said, "is what he gives. You'll get some again this evening. And every evening."

"Nothing more?"

"Fish, now and again."

"From the bay?"

He nodded. "We'll be the ones to fetch it and only if he lets us."

We went forth to work, hoes in hand. Having no choice but to deny my hunger or tiredness, I set about with my hoe as did Bara. He worked with care and I did my best to imitate what he did. All the while he continued to instruct me so I learned the work to tedious perfection.

The day remained wet and only a little less chilly though my labors had made me somewhat warm. I was full of questions, about Bara, his life, Fitzhugh, and what to expect on this small plantation. I chose however to wait for him to speak, being timid about doing or saying anything that might hinder his friendship or, worse, turn him against me.

As I was working, I chanced to notice a half-inch six-legged beetle, its round back mottled brown and black. It had a long nose such as I had never seen on an insect. On my knees I observed its slow progress. "What's this?" I called out.

Bara came and looked. "Big nose weevil," he said.

I prodded the creature with a finger and watched as it moved faster.

That's when I heard Bara suddenly say, "Get up."

I jumped only to see that Fitzhugh had crept up on us. It was almost as if he had waited for me to have paused working. In his hand was a wooden rod. His pistol was in his belt. So was a knife.

I snatched up my hoe and resumed working.

The old man stood in silence, but when I peeked behind, the frown on his face suggested he was finding grievous fault. Moreover, I sensed it was me he considered most closely.

Sure enough, he called out: "You, Oliver, you're doing that wrong."

I stopped my work and looked round. I had no idea what I was doing wrong, and therefore had no notion as to what might be the proper way. When he gave no instruction, I looked to Bara for guidance, but he continued to work without a glance in my direction. Even so, I was sure he understood what was happening.

I turned to Fitzhugh. "What . . . what do you wish me to do, sir?"

He lifted his rod and pointed. "Against that tree."

Uneasy, I stole another squint at Bara. That time, he peeped up. I was sure I detected a small movement of his head, which I decided meant, "Do as he says."

Now alarmed, but with no true grasp as to what was unfolding, I did as I was bid.

"Take off your jerkin," Fitzhugh ordered. "Back to me."

Beginning to comprehend what was about to occur, I appealed to Bara with yet another look, a frightened one.

"He won't help you," the old man called out. "Do as you're told."

Then he proclaimed: "You're my property. I can do with you what I want." That said, he flexed the rod in one hand, put his other hand on his pistol butt, and advanced. By then his meaning was all too clear.

Trembling, heart pounding, I took off my shirt and stood against the tree, the bark chafing my thin, bare chest. Even so I tried to see what he was doing. No sooner did I do that than he drew close, braced his legs, and used the rod to flog me fiercely across my back.

The pain was as if a bolt of lightning cut through my body. I gasped for breath. My knees buckled. I began to cry.

He gave me five lashes. By the fifth, if I had not been leaning against the tree I would have fallen to the ground.

Fitzhugh stopped. "Keep to work," he cried, "or it will go worse for you." Then he added, "Bara will do nothing to stop me or help you." Without another word, he went off.

For some dazed, unbearable moments, I remained leaning against the tree. Benumbed by the blows and throbbing pain, I struggled to recover my breath. I was helpless, angry, and mortified all at once. The words "You're my property. I can do with you what I want" echoed and re-echoed in my head.

Let it be said: To suffer unjust punishment in silence is to fall into a pit of fury. Make someone feel helpless and he will become helpless and, even worse, believe it.

Though my back still burned, I found strength enough to push myself from the tree.

Bara said, "Turn round. Let me see."

I did so.

"Bad," he said.

I reached behind. My touch smarted. I felt a slippery wetness. When I looked at my fingers I saw blood.

Bara turned from me and lifted his shirt. What I saw was that his back was marked with stripes and welts: signs of much flogging. There was also a scar on the right side of his neck, another on the left side. On one shoulder a burn mark.

I understood: Fitzhugh had beaten and abused him many times much the same way. I could only guess what made the other scars and burn.

Bara said, "He wanted to show you what he could do. If you're wondering why I did nothing, he's a man who becomes enraged at resistance. He wants you to fight back so he can beat you down the more."

"How . . . how have you survived?" I stammered.

Not answering, Bara threw down his hoe and said, "Follow me." He headed off in a westerly direction.

My whole body throbbing and burning so that I could barely stand, I held back. "Where you going?" I called.

"Just come."

I looked to where Fitzhugh had gone. "Won't he mind?"

"He's taught his day's lesson. He'll spend his time with drink."

Struggling with rage and misery, I smeared my tears, took a deep breath, and trudged after Bara, my eyes on his heels, limping along as best I could. Every step gave a jolting hurt.

We walked for perhaps a third of a mile.

When at last Bara stopped, I came up to his side. Only then did I raise my head and look about. What lay before me was something such as I had never seen before: the swamp.

CHAPTER THIRTY-SIX

In Which I Look upon the Strangest World.

No matter where I gazed, all I saw was still water, water the color of thin blood, even as the air was tinted green. No sky, only a high roof of interwoven branches growing from gigantic trees—some five feet round—of reddish hue, branches thick with countless needles. Dark green bushes, reedy grasses, vines, and floating plants were below, while here and there white and red flowers grew along with plants with tufted ends. Oddest of all were countless woody points, which poked up and out of the murky water. It was as if an army stood submerged, and all that remained were the visible tips of their spears.

I smelled the dampness of universal decay. I heard a constant soft gargle of water, plus the steady hum of little flying creatures, and now and again the chirp of unseen birds.

At the base of the gigantic trees, which I came to learn were called cypress, were what seemed like bloated, fluted hands—I hardly know how else to describe them—fingers of root that reached into the murky waters, as if seeking to grasp whatever lay beneath. Elsewhere, countless rotting logs, impossible to know if floating or resting on some unseen bottom.

Swarms of insects flew about, among them a kind of glittering needle. On the water surface, bubbles broke, suggesting something lived below.

Birds appeared, the most striking a bright golden color. A spotted turtle sat motionless on a floating log. A large black snake appeared, wiggling sinuously across the water, head up, hook-like.

I started back.

"Cottonmouth," said Bara. "If it bites, you're dead."

I heard a terrible roar.

"What's that?" I cried.

"Big cat," said Bara. "Probably smells us." He said it as if the beast was only to be expected.

I said, "Are you trying to frighten me?"

"Just so you know you don't want to go in there without a gun or knife."

Red mud oozed between our toes, making a gross sucking sound when we moved. Indeed, when I chanced to shift my foot my leg sank down, as if being swallowed.

Along with fresh alarm, the effort to extricate my foot brought back sharp pain.

Bara bent down and scooped up a handful of red mud. "Turn your back to me," he said. When I did, he smeared the mud over the bloody welts that came from the beating.

At first it stung, enlarging the pain, but it soon became cool and soothing.

"That's better," I mumbled, deeply grateful. And just as that lashing brought tears, so did Bara's kindness.

To distract myself, I looked at the swamp. Hard to say which it did more: astonish or frighten me. Was this what my messmate on the *Owners Goodwill* talked about? A way back to England?

I said, "How big is this place?"

"Don't know."

"Where does it go?"

"West."

"Would it get me to England?"

Bara gave a snort. "Why would you think that?"

"On my transport ship, someone told me that."

"He was a fool."

I tried to grasp what this swamp was. Its strangeness filled me with disquiet, enough to tell me I wanted nothing to do with it.

"Best get back to work," said Bara.

CHAPTER THIRTY-SEVEN

In Which I Run Away.

During the next two days, my pain subsided somewhat, but remained sharp enough to be a constant goad to my plan, which was to run away as soon as possible. I was convinced I could not endure another beating. I'd seen runaway notices. Had not others escaped? Why not me? Nor did I confide to Bara. I hardly knew him and didn't know if he could be trusted. Rather, during the next two days I held my thoughts and tongue and concentrated on tobacco labor.

Two nights after I had sustained the beating, my back still sore from the lashing, I forced myself to stay awake until late. From where I lay, in the loft of the house, I heard nothing but nighttime crickets and Bara's sleeping breath.

I have no idea the hour when I sat up, crawled to the

ladder, and began to descend. Halfway down, I paused and listened for sounds of the old man. His steady grunts and gargled breath informed me that he slept. My beating heart counted out my fears.

I continued down, slowly, noiselessly, until I reached the lower floor. Once there, I stood in place, waiting, very tense, my thoughts full of Moco Jack's attempted escape and wondering if my fate, for good or ill, would be the same. I also listened for any change in the old man's breath or movement.

Nothing I heard caused me to retreat.

How long it took me to cross the house floor I don't know. You may be sure I did so with utmost caution, hands before me, feeling the untouchable darkness, my breathing soft and shallow.

My fingers found the door. I unlatched it. My way now clear, I eased it open, so its groan was slight, then stepped outside, shutting the door behind me almost without sound.

Standing beyond the house, I took a deep breath. The air was mild, scented by living things. Easeful light came from the low, sickle-shaped moon and stars, which sparked the sky. My relief was intense, my heart pounding. Hardly a wonder: This was the first moment after many months that I was truly free. My sense of liberty was such that I wished only for wings that I might fly through the nighttime air and perch upon the moon, free of the earth.

That said, I was not so water-witted as to think I could make my way to complete freedom in such darksomeness. My plan—such as I had formed it—was to get sufficiently away from the house, wait for the first blush of dawn, and then move north as fast as my legs would take me. First, however, I allowed myself to become accustomed to the outside gloom, trying to gain some sense of the land—and steady my pounding heart.

After some moments, I began to walk toward the only way I knew, to those places where Bara and I had been seeding. I reached them easily enough. From there, I moved in the direction of the swamp since once again I knew that way. I was willing to be pursued, knowing I could not go far in that direction, but no one need know. Let them suppose I went into the swamp and perished. It seemed a likely outcome.

It wasn't long before I sensed I was approaching the swamp; not so much by sight, but by the ground becoming soft and wet beneath my bare feet. The air was dank.

I listened intently. A frog croaked. The hum and buzz of insects grew. Some animal barked or growled, a reminder which way not to go. I also thought about that snake.

When I got as near to the swamp as I dared, I turned

to what I judged northward, moving slowly, since this was land I did not know. Indeed, after going for a brief time, I paused. Not only was I now unfamiliar with the place; it was all deep murk and I did not wish to put myself in greater jeopardy than I already was. The night's chill and my tension had me trembling.

Dizzy with the lack of slumber and constant soreness, reminding myself I had not slept, I rested my arms against a tree, put my head on them, and forced myself to wait until further light. But then my eyes closed. I fell asleep.

How long I slept I don't know, but woke with a jolt, all too aware of the danger in which I'd placed myself. A red-edged dawn glowed to the east. The light, though faint, allowed me to perceive the land that lay before me, a world of mostly shadow, an intermingling of blacks and grays. The brightest thing was an eddying, ashen fog, which rolled upon the ground before me, rather like an earth-clinging cloud. I listened hard, but heard nothing save the shift of leaves bestirred by placid breezes.

An owl hooted. It did not bother me. I also heard what sounded like a breaking branch. Alarmed, that time I waited. I recalled Bara's words about needing a knife. I wished I had one. When the sound was not repeated, I willed myself to believe no one was about and that I had no need of weapons. I was free. Just not free enough.

Go on, I told myself.

My eyes adjusted to the slowly brightening light.

In the open space before me, a mound rose rather like a bulging bubble of earth. Its modest peak was cresting above the mist, so that—I thought—if I stood on it, I might see farther, and thereby seek a safe line of escape.

I went on with care, my bare feet sinking slightly, making a slight sucking sound each time I lifted them: Was I too close to the swamp? I paused briefly then pushed on, wading through the white vapor, heading for that mound.

I reached it, then climbed with ease to its top. But no sooner did I reach the small summit than the earth gave way, and I plunged into a pit, down as far as my chest.

First came the shock of the sudden drop. Next came relief that I had not been hurt.

As my breath recovered, I looked about. Dawn had strengthened enough for me to see where I had fallen. That was when I realized I was surrounded by human bones, including a human head to which skin and hair was still attached. The jaw was open, so it seemed to be screaming. The stench was revolting.

I had fallen into a new grave.

My heart all but bursting in my chest, I fairly leaped out of the pit. Once on top, I peered down. I saw decayed flesh and shreds of what must have been clothing. It was a human—a boy by the looks of him—a Negro.

On the instant, my thoughts went to that murdered

boy, Clark. What had Fitzhugh said of him? "Never got off my land."

Here—I had no doubt—he was.

My will to escape shrank to nothing and was replaced by terror. Too frightened to go on, I all but flew back to Fitzhugh's house. Breathing deep and fast, heart atumble, I snatched up a hoe that was leaning against the building and held it across my heaving chest, as if I could ward off horror with it.

Eyes squeezed tight so as to blot away the dreadfulness of what I'd seen, my thoughts were spiraling. I knew nothing of Clark, save that he was a boy like me who had tried to run away. Even so, I was engulfed by anguish for him while simultaneously understanding that Fitzhugh was nothing less than a monster.

I do not consider myself irrational, but I could not muster the thought of fleeing in that northerly direction. Or any other way. It was as if that ghastly grave had turned into many graves and extended across all the land. I was sure there was no way to escape.

None.

CHAPTER THIRTY-EIGHT

In Which I Receive a Spark of Hope.

Full dawn bloomed in reds, purples, and pinks. Feeling ill, I remained sitting against the house until Bara opened the door and came out. The sound made me start, but my relief was great. I looked up at him, knowing all my sadness and shame must have been revealed in my imploring eyes.

He gazed at me, but said nothing. Though I could not read his face, I had no doubt he knew I had tried to escape. After a moment, still not speaking, he took up the other hoe and started off to the fields.

I got up and followed him.

"What about the hogs?" I said.

"For once, they can wait."

It was only when we'd gone some ways from the house—out of Fitzhugh's hearing distance—that Bara halted, placed a hand on my shoulder, looked me straight in the face, and said, "What made you come back?"

"I . . . I fell into a grave."

That took him by surprise.

I said, "I think . . . I think it's that Clark."

"Show me."

I led him to where I'd been.

Bara gazed into the pit. He was breathing hard.

I whispered, "Is it him?"

Bara continued to stare down. His face was tight, as if he were clenching his teeth. Abruptly, he turned from me and covered his face with his hands. His shoulders jerked. He dropped to his knees and crossed his hands over his chest, as if hugging himself. His body rocked slightly.

I wanted to comfort him. "Bara . . ." I said.

He shook his head, letting me know he did not want me to say a word.

After some while he stood up.

"I'm sorry," I said.

"You could cover the world with ten feet of sorry, wouldn't make a difference." Then he said, "We'd better put it the way it was. Don't want the old man to know we found it. No telling what he'd do."

In silence, we filled the grave.

Afterward, still not talking, we went to where we were meant to be weeding the tobacco field and set to with our hoes. Bara still said nothing but when I glanced at him I saw tears run down his face.

I said, "He was your friend, wasn't he?"

Bara nodded. He seemed to be struggling for words. Only after some while did he say, "Fitzhugh beat him the way he did me, and you. One time when it was worse than ever, Clark screamed at him, 'I won't stay. I won't stay.'

"Next day he was gone. I guessed, but didn't know what happened. I'd warned him. He wouldn't listen. I was hoping he got away."

I waited for Bara to speak again. It took some moments, during which he wiped more tears away.

"Hope you've learned something," he finally said. "You can try going, but it's near impossible going off by yourself. Too many dangers for one. If we're going to go, it has to be both of us."

"Do you want to leave?"

"You think I want to be here?" he said. There was contempt in his voice. "I was hoping to go with Clark. You saw how far he got. Then I was wishing Fitzhugh would get someone big and strong. He got you."

"I'll get bigger," I told him. It must have sounded woeful.

"Have to wait, won't I?" After a moment Bara said, "But we can't just go running off. Has to be the right time. Right way. Right plan."

"Where would we go?"

"Swamp."

"*Swamp?*" I cried. When my messmate Rufus Caulwell had described it to me on the boat, it seemed so fantastical I did not believe him. Now that I'd seen it with my own eyes, foul-smelling, thick with snakes and other creatures, it may have been real, but it was loathsome.

I said, "Have you gone into it?"

"Some."

"How far?"

"Enough."

"Enough for what?"

He didn't answer.

"Why are you telling me about it?"

"You asked how we can survive."

I shook my head. "I can't go in there. I'll find another way."

He said, "There is no other way. All the colonies have slaves and convicts. To get free you have to go through the swamp."

I said nothing.

"It goes on for miles. Westward. A whole world of it. In there, somewhere, are slaves, like me, bound servants, and convicts, like you. Least, that's what I've been told. Those people run off and live, in deep, secret places, places that people like Fitzhugh can't get to.

"Those people do more than hide. They set up living places. Stay there for years. Even raise up children."

"Who told you about it?"

"Other slaves. In Annapolis. The people that get there, they're called maroons."

"Why that?"

"Not sure. I just know they live there. Free."

"Have you ever seen them?"

He shook his head. "Too far in. And it's secret. Because magistrates and people like Fitzhugh, they're always trying to catch them. So those people have to be watchful. No, I haven't seen them. But I believe it. That's where I'm going. Thing is," Bara added, "you have to know how to get through."

"How?"

He looked downhill, toward the house where Fitzhugh was presumably still sleeping.

"Come on. Be quick. I'll show you."

Running, we reached the swamp. Bara said, "You asked me how we can get through." He bent down and picked up two stones. They were somewhat round and flat. "They look the same?"

"Mostly."

He handed one to me. "Let's see how far you can throw it."

I threw the stone into the water. It landed a short way off, making a watery plop.

Bara took his stone, and with a side motion, flung it out. To my surprise, the stone skipped over the water surface some ten times, going much farther than mine had.

I said, "How'd you do that?"

"Takes time to learn. Just know, if you go there"—he nodded toward the swamp—"you'll need to learn how to skip over it—like that stone. We better get back. He'll be up soon."

We hurried back to the field. Soon as we got there, Bara began to chop at the ground with his hoe. I went on my knees, pulled weeds, and softened the earth by some tobacco shoots. After some time, I said, "Bara, if you go, will you let me come with you?"

"Have to see what you are, don't I? Need to see how smart you are. Not doing what you did this morning."

"Teach me."

"First thing, you have to be patient. Start with that. Can you?"

"I promise."

"The way I see it we'll have only one chance. We either get free, or not. Best time is after summer, when the swamp waters go down."

"That's months."

"That's what is. But no talking about it. Don't even think it. Forget everything I said. If he"—I knew he meant Fitzhugh—"guesses one word, one thought, we're done. Like Clark."

"I understand."

"You'd better. I can't protect you. No more than I could protect Clark. He was a fool to go alone. Fools don't live long. We either go together and live or stay here and die."

I believed Bara. I just had to wait. Then we would go. Into the swamp. Together.

CHAPTER THIRTY-NINE

In Which I Tell You What My Days Were Like.

Recall that my mother died a few hours after I was born. Since my father did not remarry and had no more than a shrubby interest in being paternal, I was for the most part raised by my elder sister, Charity.

It was my experience then to be guided and protected by someone not much older than me. Thus, when Charity took herself to London, her going altered my life. Without her I felt abandoned. Yes, my sister and I were briefly reunited, but my misfortunes in England came about in large measure because of my urgent want of Charity's guidance and therefore my search for her.

It was easy then, for me to accept Bara—who was also somewhat older than me—as my teacher, companion, and protector. Add to that my great dread of Fitzhugh, and you will grasp my need to follow Bara in everything. I took to him as if he were my older, knowing brother who always wished things to be done right. Yes, he had no desire to incur the old man's vile anger, but mostly, he took pride in his work. I wanted to do well too, to earn Bara's respect.

That said, I beg you, do not think of us as two playful boys. We were laboring servants, working from early light to late shadows. The names of days—Monday, Thursday—meant nothing. Every day was yesterday. Tomorrow would become yesterday. Nor did I count weeks or measure months. The days grew hotter, wetter, and ever wearier. Monotony was our portion. Besides the tobacco plants we were also required to take care of the horse and hogs. To cook our daily food.

The only change for Bara and me came about when there was rain. On such days, we pounded corn kernels into the meal we ate, a hard and drearisome task.

We never knew when Fitzhugh spied on us. Never knew when he would beat us. He did so three more times to Bara, the same to me. No reasons—as if any reasons could justify such evil acts—were ever given. The pain was great. The degradation extreme. Our rage was high but—of necessity—held within. There is no greater pain than a pain held within. But shared pain is somewhat lesser pain.

Fearful that Fitzhugh would overhear us, Bara and I never talked much. Rather we were silent together and communicated in other ways, looks, gestures. Our eyes spoke and served—along with swamp mud—as balm.

Meanwhile, the old man was more often than not swashed with drink, though where he purchased his liquor, I don't know. I only knew he consumed it constantly. As far as I could see, my awful life would remain the same until Bara told me otherwise.

CHAPTER FORTY

In Which I Share What I Learned about Bara.

Though Bara remained in many ways unknown to me, I came to trust him and looked to him for direction, of which I had vast need. Hardly a surprise I came to love him as a brother. That said, whereas it is not uncommon for older brothers to overlord their younger siblings, that was not the case with Bara. But reserve was Bara's armor. Endurance was his strength. Considering my deep ignorance, my demonstrated folly, he was more than kind. Indeed, he proved generous.

As time passed, our brotherhood enlarged, and when Fitzhugh was around, Bara and I learned to communicate with our eyes, merely by looking at each other. One look said, "Yes." Another "no." Another look said, "Be careful." And much more complex notions, which I have not the language to express. He had told me I must be patient, and I was determined to be that.

One day, when we were working in the tobacco fields, Bara abruptly said, "Who is Charity?"

That took me by surprise. "How do you know about her?"

"In your sleep last night, you spoke the name."

"She's my sister."

"Where is she?"

"Do you truly want to know about her? About me?"

He said, "If you wish to tell me."

I related my story much as I have expressed it on these pages, though much abridged. He listened as we continued to work but said not one word. I even shared my lace piece with him.

When I had related my tale, he said, "You care to know who I am?" It was as if we were exchanging gifts.

"Yes, please."

"The furthest back I can remember," Bara began, "I was on an island. Barbados, I think. Where English people rule. I was born there, a slave. I have no memory of my father. If I think about my mother, she's but blurry. From Africa, I believe. Guinea I was told. I have no idea if they still live, and if so, where. I don't know who gave me my name. I hope it's what my parents gave me. An Afric name. That name Bara is the only thing I own.

"I don't know if I have brothers, sisters. Or any relations. My family was those with whom I lived and worked, fellow slaves. My oldest memories are constant work with sugarcane: digging cane holes, planting, trashing, cutting, tying, loading, carting. Great heat, little food, and punishments for not working more. Many died.

"I know who I am, but not a day passes when I do not wonder who else might know me. I never spent a day in school. I can't read or write.

"One day, very young, I was herded off with other slaves, brought to Annapolis, and sold to an Englishman, a government official. I worked from dawn until night as a house servant in his home, one of a number of slaves. One of my tasks was waiting on table and Mistress insisted I learn to speak as they spoke. Dressed me fine, even to a wig to impress her guests. I guess it was the rage in England to have young black boys wait on tables.

"But then they went back to England. I didn't know why. When they went they sold their slaves. Being so young, no one wanted me. Not for field work. It was Fitzhugh who—for a bargain—bought me. I've been here, I believe, two years."

I took all that in and thought about it. A day later, as we were working, I said, "You've been a good teacher. But there's one thing I can do that you can't."

"What?"

"I can read and write. I could teach you."

"How?"

With the hoe handle I scratched out the letter B.

"What's that?"

"B. The first letter of your name." I said the letter. "B. Buh. Bara."

After looking about to make sure Fitzhugh was not near, Bara squatted down beneath the tobacco leaves, and with a finger copied the letter. "B," he said, looking up at me for confirmation.

I nodded.

Then I scratched out the rest of his name. A R A.

"That's your name," I said. I said each of the letters, and then his name. He repeated it all with me. We did so a number of times.

I stepped away. For a long time, he stared at the name and letters. Then his fingers moved over the letters, as if feeling his own name. He also said the name aloud any number of times. Spelled it out.

For the rest of the day we worked with our hoes in silence. But every now and again Bara paused, bent over, and wrote his name in the dirt, saying it, only to erase it.

One time he pointed to himself and said, "Bara. B, A, R, A."

Every day I taught Bara new letters. He learned well. Since there was not a page to read (and if there was, it would not have been safe to try) I taught him how to spell and read names. My own. Fitzhugh. Charity. Clark. Then things. Tobacco. Hoe. Dirt. Water. And any other thing he asked for.

It may seem little enough, but it came to be that Bara's knowledge of reading altered everything.

CHAPTER FORTY-ONE

Excursion upon the Bay, Wherein a Fish Is Caught and a Runaway Plan Is Prepared.

I t was late summer. I cannot tell you just when. The heat was extreme, more than I ever believed it could be. The heavy, damp air clung like sheets of lead. Breathing was hard. We shared no talk of escaping, none. But I have no doubt it was always in Bara's mind, as it was in mine.

In the meantime, Bara and I worked all day, every day. Our whole labor was given mostly to tobacco. By this time the plants had grown four to seven feet tall, with large, fanlike leaves. The crop had grown enough that although the actual ingathering was still some time off, Bara was able to estimate what the harvest would be. In answer to Fitzhugh's persistent questions, he shared that guess with the old man. To show his satisfaction, Fitzhugh said, "I haven't eaten fish in a long time. I want you to get some tomorrow." With a nod toward me, he added, "Take him. I'll give you the paddle and spear."

These tools, I soon learned, were things he kept in his locked chest.

The next day after work—the twilight sky summer soft—Bara and I went to the shore of the bay. He held out a thick pole, with one end flat and wider than the rest. "A paddle," he informed me. "It moves a canoe."

"Canoe?" I said.

"You'll see."

In his other hand, Bara carried a slender rod that had at one end a sharp iron tip, the tip having a barb. At the other end a cord was attached.

"What's that?" I asked.

"Fish spear."

On the bay edge of Fitzhugh's land, a small wharf had been constructed, which looked to have been made from cypress logs driven into soft earth, then covered with planks. I had seen it on my first day, but never dared to venture near. You may recall the old man had forbidden me to go there.

As for the canoe, it was stowed on the ground near this wharf. As best as I could tell it was made from a hollowed-out cypress log, dark red, some eighteen feet in length.

The two of us brought it from the land to the water. Once afloat, it was easeful to move. Still, I eyed it with disquiet. "Are we getting in that?"

"Have to."

"I can't swim."

"I can. I'll teach you. You'll need to know." Bara handed me the pointed spear and cord. "Wait here," he said.

As I looked on, he waded into the bay up to his waist, bent over, and seemed to be feeling down into the water. What he pulled up were five stone-like objects, which he threw on the land where I was standing. They were rough, knurly things, about twelve inches in length, and as much as four inches wide. To my eyes, they looked like encrusted stones.

"What's that?" I called.

"Oysters."

Back on land, Bara smashed two of these rocklike things together. What I took to be stones were shells and they shattered. To my surprise, he scooped out the innards, and to my further astonishment, put the gob into his mouth.

He broke open another and plopped a wet hunk into my hand. It was slimy and smelled repulsive.

"Go on," urged Bara. "Eat it."

I stared at the mess.

"Eat it," he commanded. For once he was grinning.

I forced myself to eat, and when I did, it took effort not to retch.

My reaction was one of the few times when I saw Bara actually giggle. "You can live on them." His expression became serious again. "It's something you should learn. You can read words. You need to read the world. When you can, you're ready to be free."

Before I could respond he said, "Get in the canoe, but sit low, or it'll roll over. Then you'll swim or drown."

We pushed the canoe into the water. The little boat seemed perilously unstable. On the instant, I recalled that saying: "He who is born to be drowned will never be hanged." You may be sure that I clung to the sides of the canoe, and felt my stomach lurch with each roll.

Bara, who continued to be amused by my discomfort, took up the paddle and used it to shift us farther out into the bay.

As we moved over the water, I looked back and saw Fitzhugh. He had come down to the wharf, musket in hand. As always, he was watching us. "Not too far," he called.

Bara, not looking in my direction when he spoke, said, "Don't talk loud. Sound goes far across water."

"How far can he shoot?" I said.

"Far enough. If he sees us talk, he'll want to know what we said. When you speak, turn from shore. Let him only see the back of your head."

"Couldn't we keep going?"

"My color," he said. "Your collar."

Bara propelled the canoe farther out. When we had gone some ways into the bay, he took to peering into the water.

"What are you trying to see?" I asked.

"All kinds of fish here: mullets, sturgeon, plaice. I'd like to get us a sturgeon. Big fish. The bigger the fish the more likely we'll get to eat some.

"Sturgeons sleep on the bottom during the day. When evening comes, they wake up, get near the surface."

Bara kept staring into the water. "No talking," he said. He handed the paddle to me. "Learn to use it," he said.

I imitated what I'd seen him do, and found I could guide the canoe with little trouble. We moved about for I don't know how long. Now and again I glanced back to the shore. Fitzhugh continued to stand there, watching us intently, musket in hand.

We floated quietly, Bara gazing down into the water.

But then, without turning in my direction, as if talking into the water, he said, "Are you willing to run away soon?"

"I . . . I want to," I managed to reply.

"Need to wait some for the water to go down in the swamp. But before heavy rains come."

On the instant, that place, the swamp—land indistinguishable from water, green air, gigantic cypress trees, snakes, and other hidden beasts—bloomed as an awful vision in my mind.

"It's dareful," continued Bara as if he saw my thoughts. "But, I told you, it's the only way." He was staring down. As he spoke, he had that pole with the iron tip in his hand pointed toward the water. Without looking at me he said, "Just have to wait for the best time."

"But—" I glanced back toward shore, to see Fitzhugh still standing on watch.

With a sudden thrust of his arm, Bara plunged the pole down. "Got him," he cried, let go of the pole, and grabbed the cord, which became taut.

"Need your help," he called.

I edged closer to him—the canoe rocking dangerously—and grabbed hold of the cord with both hands. The cord seemed alive, lugging and twisting, with what felt like a great weight attached.

"Don't pull at it," said Bara. "Let him exhaust himself."

I followed what Bara did, sometimes easing out the line, sometimes hauling it in. Gradually, I began to see what appeared to be a silvery thing of great size beneath us. It was turning and twisting and the water turned red with blood.

The fish continued to thrash about, gradually rising to the surface, until it floated—white belly turned to the side—giving the appearance that it had died.

"Hold the cord," Bara said.

That I did while he reached into the water, and using all his strength, hauled up a gigantic gray fish—some four feet in length. It had a sharp, flat nose, and bumps along its spine.

"Sturgeon," said Bara.

Dumped into the bottom of the canoe, the fish thrashed about a bit.

"Be careful of his teeth," Bara warned. Then he used the paddle to subdue it.

After removing the sharp pole from the sturgeon's flesh, he grasped the now-dead creature with two hands and held it up so Fitzhugh could see it. At the same moment, not looking at me, he said, "You truly willing to go?"

Of course, I wished to go, but escaping through the swamp filled me with unease. All I could say was, "Do you know the way?"

"Think so."

"Where would it take us?"

"Far enough." On Fitzhugh's nod, Bara dropped the fish into the canoe. "Will you?" he pressed.

Of course, I was eager to flee. But I feared I had neither the skill nor the strength to get away from Fitzhugh's violence or get through the swamp. Afraid to tell Bara of my worries, all I did was nod.

Bara said, "It's like catching that fish. You wait. You look. You see. You strike. You avoid his teeth." After a pause he added, "Be ready. A few more dry weeks are all we need."

"Do we have to do anything to get ready?"

"I'll do what I have to do. You do what you need to do."

"What do you mean?"

"Getting through the swamp will be hard, but don't think I'm going to take care of you. You'll have to take care of yourself. Sure, we'll help each other, but you must keep getting stronger, smarter. Don't let the old man notice anything or we'll be dead."

It was I who awkwardly paddled the canoe back to the little wharf. Bara returned the paddle and spear to Fitzhugh, who placed them in his chest and clicked the lock closed.

Never mind: In a few weeks Bara and I would flee. Patience, I told myself. Patience.

CHAPTER FORTY-TWO

A Mysterious Occurrence in the Night.

That night, in unusual jovial spirits—while eating all the fish—Fitzhugh made an announcement: he would go to Annapolis the next day.

"My credit is low," he said. "With the crop figured, I can meet with my factor."

Though I didn't know what he meant I didn't ask.

Fitzhugh drank even more than usual. As the darkness increased, he grew increasingly jumbled and excited. At one point, he threw down the two knives with which he had been working onto the table and shouted, "Repel all attacks," although such sieges were advancing only in his drunkenship. He even pulled up his pistol and shot into the ceiling. In that little space the sound was deafening and terrifying.

Though greatly alarmed, I, seated with my back

against the wall, merely looked on. If Bara had reactions like mine, he didn't dare express them either.

After yet more drinking, Fitzhugh rose up and cried out to us, "Off with you."

Relieved to be dismissed, Bara and I climbed to the loft, where we lay down in the suffocating heat, listening to Fitzhugh stumbling about in his soggy stupor.

"He knows money is coming," whispered Bara. "It's the only thing that makes him more excited than drink." After a few moments, he added, "It will be a deep sleep." After another pause: "I don't think he reloaded his pistol."

Sure enough, it was not long before Master's mutters became the rumbles of his deep sleep.

"What," I whispered, "did he mean by a factor?"

"He's the man who takes the tobacco and arranges to sell it in England. Mr. Lunbog. I've gone to meet him with Fitzhugh a few times. Now that the old man knows what the tobacco crop will be, he'll work out a contract with Lunbog. You heard him: he needs credit."

I made no response, but Bara seemed more alert than usual. He was thinking hard about something. I did not ask what, just watched.

At some point, in such moonlight that came through the cracks in the loft walls, I saw Bara sit up.

"What is it?"

"Shhh . . ."

He listened awhile then rolled upon his knees.

"What are you doing?"

"Stay here," he said.

I saw Bara move toward the ladder, swing about, and start to go down. Though I had done the same thing within days of my arrival, I now understood the risk much more. This was most dangerous behavior. What if he was caught? If a struggle ensued, what should I do? I could only hope Fitzhugh was truly, deeply asleep.

I crawled to the edge of the hole from which the ladder dropped and peered into the lower darkness to see what transpired. Bara was standing on the main floor as if waiting. Then he began to move toward the table.

There was light enough to see the glint of metal. When abed, Fitzhugh normally put the pistol by his side. That time, in his stupor he had left it on the table. Next to it lay the knives with which he had been working.

With small, silent steps, Bara stretched out his hand over the table and then withdrew. The pistol remained.

I watched as Bara crept toward the door, unlatched and opened it—soundlessly—and then stepped outside.

I was fairly wild to follow and learn what he was doing. It even came to my mind that he might be running off without me. Withal, I told myself to trust him, and forced myself not to move, but gave myself over to the deepest listening, watching.

At first I perceived nothing, but then I heard the hogs grunting. Those sounds did not last long. I kept listening.

To my great relief, the door eased open. Bara returned. With a few quiet steps, he was back on the ladder and in the loft.

"What did you do?" I said in as small a voice as I could muster.

"Can't say."

"Why?"

"If you don't know, Fitzhugh won't be able to beat it out of you."

Bara rolled over and fell asleep.

Patience, I told myself repeatedly, until I too fell asleep. Patience.

In the morning Fitzhugh—along with Bara and me—departed for his meeting with his factor in Annapolis. It was there that once again my life changed unexpectedly.

CHAPTER FORTY-THREE

What Befell Us in Annapolis.

The next day arrived hot and humid. The sky was musty gray, the forest greenery through which we passed thick, glossy, and drooping. A heavy promise of rain prevailed. But it was fine not to be working in the fields.

Fitzhugh was on his horse, while Bara and I walked before him. The old man was dressed in his usual unkempt, dirty garb. As for Bara and me, we wore our normal ragged clothing, our feet bare. Surely, we were a derelict trio.

The route we traversed was the same that I had walked months before when first I came, crossing over two rivers by ferryboats. Of course, instead of going north, we traveled south. When we passed people, Fitzhugh was no more social than before.

Unlike my first journey, no rope was attached to me,

nor was there one on Bara. The arrangement was such that Fitzhugh—his ever-ready cocked and primed pistol at his hip—could keep his distrustful eyes on us.

I was glad to travel over the road again, committing as much as I could to memory. Bara had said we would get away through the swamp. Despite my utter trust in him, the thought of that awful place still caused me much unease. Surely, I told myself, there must be a better way.

It was in late afternoon when we reached Annapolis and the Royal George, the same tavern where Fitzhugh and I stopped that day after he purchased me. Once we arrived, he led us directly to the stable, where he tied up his horse. "Stay here till I tell you otherwise."

He left us.

If you wonder why we—left unattended—did not break away, I will remind you again of vital things. There is a habit of servitude, and it comes from the real fear of being disciplined ruthlessly. That fear of punishment often becomes a kind of punishment. One lives in a state of perpetual cowering—or least one acted so. It fended off cruelty. Thus, we remained in the stable.

There was much more: Bara, being black, could have been stopped by any white man demanding to know who he was, where he came from, and whether he had written permission to wander.

And I, though white, still had my iron collar round my

neck, which made me an equal mark for anyone who chose to stop and apprehend me since I, too, needed written consent to walk free. Indeed, for both of us the risk of being caught, and the resulting penalty and punishments, were enough to keep us in place.

But why, you might ask, since I could write, did I not compose counterfeit permission letters? I beg you: Where was I to find pen, ink, and paper? Common things indeed, but given our circumstance, impossible to be found. I have already told you about Fitzhugh's mark when he signed my bill of sale with an *X*. I don't believe he could read or write and therefore had no use for pen or paper. Regardless, I had no idea what to write in such a permission letter.

As we continued to sit there in the stable, I was pleased to see the same young serving girl who had been kind to me when I'd first been at the tavern. She was bringing us a corn loaf and some cider.

At first, she did not recognize me, but merely said, "Your master sent you this."

As we took the food I said, "You've forgotten me."

She looked at me with puzzlement.

"Fitzhugh's felon," I explained. "I stopped here the first day he purchased me. You spoke kindly. And this is Bara, my friend."

The girl offered both of us a kindly smile and to me asked, "How have you fared?"

"We've survived," I said.

To prove she truly did recall me, she added, "Did you ever find your sister?"

"Not yet," I said.

"I hope you will. A good night to you both."

For a moment after she left us, we sat in silence. I asked, "Do you think you might ever find your family?"

"Don't know who they are, or what they look like. Not even their names." That rarity: his voice was sad.

I think it was only then I fully understood how companionless Bara was. "Have you any notion where to search?"

He remained silent. By that time, I had learned that when he didn't answer, it was because he was thinking how to respond. So it was after some time had passed that he said, "I know where I intend to look."

I said, "The swamp? Those maroons?"

"It's not that I don't wish to tell you," he said. "It's what I've told you before. Fitzhugh might beat it out of you. If you don't know, you can't tell him. Same as I said before: it will be safer that way."

Such was our world that I understood him.

We continued sitting in silence, each with our own thoughts. Outside, and inside the stable, it had grown to dusk, the air heavier still. At a distance, thunder growled.

Bara stood up.

"Where you going?"

"Out. Before it rains."

He left the stable. Tired, I settled back. When Bara returned, he stood before me.

"What is it?"

"I was trying to read the notices outside the tavern."

"Could you?"

"Some." His voice dropped to a whisper. "On one of them I read had your sister's name: Charity."

"Are you sure?" I cried.

"You taught me to read, didn't you?"

I jumped up and hurried out through the stable door, ready to retreat if anyone appeared, and went directly to that board where many notices were posted. In the dim light, I looked over them. One read:

In search of Oliver Cromwell Pitts; a transported felon from London. Aged twelve. Believed to have been sent to North America. If any information found about him please inform the Bakery of Master Isaac Bell, Black Horse Alley in city of Philadelphia. High reward. His sister, Mistress Charity Pitts.

I think my heart stopped beating.

CHAPTER FORTY-FOUR

My Search for Philadelphia.

I beg you to understand: it was almost as if Bara—and therefore I—after so long a time, loss, and hope, had found Charity. As if she were standing there right before me.

At first, I did no more than read and reread the notice. Every time I read it, I was filled with increasing excitement. I actually spoke the words of the posting aloud, stumbling only on "Philadelphia," since the word being new to me.

As I read my thoughts cascaded:

Charity had survived.

She was somewhere.

She was looking for me.

She would rescue me.

I would find her.

Beyond all else, I would be with her.

But alas, she was not there. She was in some place called Philadelphia, of which I had no notion any more than I could say it. Was it near or far?

My sense of urgency was immediate: I must find out where it was and go to her.

Except, it took but a moment for me to realize I could do none of the things I desired. Never mind that I did not know where this Philadelphia was. I was forbidden to go so much as one step without permission.

I returned to the stable.

My emotions must have been writ large on my face because Bara needed but one look at me before he said, "Was it her? Did I read it right?"

Breathless, I said, "She's looking for me. From a place called Phila . . . delphia. Bara, I have to tell her where I am. Go to her." I said this as if—for it surely felt that way to me—it was something I must do at once. "Do you know where it is?"

"Never heard of it. You can ask the servant girl."

No sooner said than I looked out through the stable door, prepared to go. Barely had I done that when Fitzhugh stumbled in, walking with the instability of excessive drink. As so often the case, he reeked of rum.

He glowered at us, but said nothing. If he noted

that I was standing, wanting to leave, he gave no sign. Instead, he tottered into the empty stall that held his horse. Once there, he piled up some hay, threw it down, and lay down.

It was clear that he was going to sleep.

Bara reached out and gripped my leg, reminding me I must wait. Though much vexed and fairly trembling with eagerness, there was nothing for me to do but retreat and sit.

We sat there waiting, listening. Bara, ever watchful, refrained from speaking. Though full of turmoil, I didn't talk either. Altogether desperate to question the tavern girl, I knew I must bide my time. When I heard thunder rumble overhead, it was as if it were an echo of my raging emotions.

Thankfully, it was not so long before I heard Fitzhugh's sleeping sounds, his mutters and growls, and now and again his snuffled snores.

Bara heard them too. He gave me a poke. I needed no further urging. We jumped up and went to the stable door, made certain no one was about, and then stepped outside, where it was dark. I had no notion as to the hour, but all seemed slumbering.

I looked to the tavern. It was completely dark. To see it so was as if a door had been shut against my face. I would not be able to speak to the girl. Exasperated to all but a rage, I tried to think where else I might have my question answered as to where Philadelphia might be. With my small knowledge of Annapolis, I could think of only one place.

"I'm going to the wharf," I announced in a whisper.

"What?"

"A seaman might know where this Philadelphia is."

"Are you in earnest? Now?"

"I have to find out."

"Oliver, it needs to wait."

"Bara," I all but shouted, "it's worth my life."

"You'll get us killed."

"I don't care. I must find out where she is."

"Don't be a fool. It's too dark. And you'll care if it goes badly."

I glanced up. The moon was peeking out from behind fast-moving clouds, but, I was sure, gave sufficient light to help me find my way.

"There's enough light," I said.

"Light enough for you to be seen."

"I'll be quick."

"You can't be fast enough."

"I will," I insisted, and moved away from the stable.

I had taken but a few steps when Bara put a hand on

my shoulder, and caused me to halt. "Just know," he said, "if the old man finds out what we're doing, it'll go terribly for us. You're doing what Clark did."

I brushed his hand away. "You said Clark was foolish. I'm not. And I can go alone."

"I shouldn't have told you about your sister. You're putting me in danger too." I heard anger in his voice. "I don't want to go into the swamp alone."

"Then stay here," I said, and caring nothing for him or his warnings, I hurried off.

CHAPTER FORTY-FIVE

In Which I Pass through Annapolis and What I Discover.

Whatever else Annapolis may have been—the seat of government—it was a drowsy place. Most buildings were dark, though here and there, wavering candlelight gleamed from cracks in shutters or poked out from under doors. As I hurried on I heard the cheerful tinkling of a harpsichord, much like a trilling bird. Far from soothing, it made me aware that people were close. Still, everything appeared calm, not a single soul abroad. I told myself that all were within. Moreover, my attentiveness months ago when I'd been led from the *Owners Goodwill* through the town to jail now served me. I had some sense as to where I was going.

There was a distant flash of lightning against the night sky, and moments later, a toss of thunder. Indeed, the night air had grown heavy enough to burst. Like my unquiet spirits. Even as I rushed on, I glanced back and saw that Bara was following me. Annoyed, wanting to show I didn't need him, I quickened my step.

All but running, I moved on, the sound of my feet slight on the dirt streets, only to observe the shape of someone coming along the street in my direction, a glowing lantern in hand. On the instant, I halted and peered into the dark.

"Who's there?" the person cried, and lifted his lantern.

I dashed into a near byway, a narrow mews, with houses close on either side. The path led I knew not where, save that it was away from the person who'd called. I rushed on. At some length, I stopped, my breathing coming hard. Then I peered back and listened.

There was no suggestion that the person—whoever it was—had followed. All was hushed.

I turned back around and made my way to the head of the mews. Once there I peeked out and saw no one. Much relieved, I continued downhill. Once, twice, I glanced back. Bara was still following me. I acted as if I hadn't noticed.

Annapolis streets are at all odd angles, but generally lead in the direction I wanted, toward water. I could still see the steeple of the town's great church silhouetted against the night sky. I kept it behind me and it wasn't long before I spied the gray bay and smelled its brine.

Within moments, I reached the head of the town's rectangular cove, the market space. Before me lay the wharf where ships were tied up, cargoes loaded and unloaded, where I had first stepped ashore. I paused to study the area.

Moonlight revealed a large ship there, her bulk looming like a vast shadow. She was a three-masted vessel, with towering masts. To my disappointment no lights were on her. She appeared deserted and would have no seaman with whom I might speak. I actually had the notion that I could steal upon her, hide and sail off. Perhaps to this Philadelphia. But what if she went back to England? I'd be hanged.

As I stood there I saw a small red light, which, as I stared, moved about up and down. After gazing for a while I realized it must be the glow of a pipe. A person was sitting on the quay next to the ship, smoking.

Now that I saw that someone was there, my hopes rekindled. I know how mad it sounds now, but in my frenzy to find Charity, nothing was going to hold me back in that moment. I was further emboldened by telling myself that no one knew me in Annapolis.

I moved along the wharf, and as I did so, the ship seemed to grow bigger. I could hear the small slap of water against her hull and the wharf, its isolation and deserted state serving only to encourage me.

A few yards from the smoking man, I stopped next to a building that cast a pool of shadow. Trusting that I was completely hidden from sight, I studied the man as the glow from his pipe bowl continued to move about. A candle lamp flickered at his feet, allowing me to see that he was sitting on some kind of bench and that he was a large man, almost bull-like in size and manner.

For a while, I stood motionless and just gazed. He was no one I knew, and accordingly, I told myself, he would not know me. I therefore stepped out from the shadows, drew nearer to the smoking man, and called out, "Sir. Please. A word."

The man turned, gazed in my direction, and in a booming voice said, "Come on then."

I drew closer. As I did, out from behind the bulk of this large man another man—a much smaller fellow—leaned forward to look at me. By the lantern light I recognized him at once: it was Mr. Sandys.

CHAPTER FORTY-SIX

Which Contains More Unexpected Things.

F ear sliced through me.

At that moment, I could have run away. Instead, I stood and told myself: I must find out about Philadelphia. It's night. I'm darker from working in the sun. I must have become taller. I am not dressed the way I was when he last saw me. Mr. Sandys will not recognize me.

Thus, not only did I stay, I moved forward.

Do you understand now the honest subtitle of my narrative?

My Follies, Fortunes & Fate

Acting as if Sandys were not there, I gave all my attention to the large man. The lantern at his feet shed enough light so I could see he was indeed a portly fellow with a great paunch. His clothing revealed a man of prosperity with fine lace at his ample sleeves and silk cloth round his neck.

His face was round, pink with fleshy, jangling jowls, a many-layered chin, and a rosebud of a mouth. Over a big wig, he wore a three-corner hat. In one large hand, he held that clay pipe from which tobacco smoke issued forth. I went so far as to decide there was something encheering in this man's appearance, rather like a plum pudding with a wig. What ill will could he possibly have toward me? I was sure he could do me no harm. I held my ground.

"Now, then, my dear boy," the fellow cried out. "What can I do for you this rain-likely evening?" He spoke slowly, articulating each word as if it was weighted—as he was in body—with large-sized importance.

"Please, sir," I said, "can you tell me where the place that goes by the name of Philadelphia might be?"

"Phil-a-del-phia?" the man echoed, pronouncing each syllable distinctly after which he drew upon his clay pipe as if I had asked him a question that required intense thought. Instead of answering me, he turned to Sandys:

"Now, sir, you are the town's watchman." He spoke as if he enjoyed the sound of his own voice. "Might you know why an offensively smelling boy in rags might be wandering about in the dark of night, asking a stranger about the city of . . . Philadelphia?"

Though afraid to look directly at him, I was aware that Mr. Sandys was regarding me with what I thought was a beam of amusement. His gaze jangled me.

"Perhaps," said Mr. Sandys, "he wishes to go there. Pray tell, Mr. Lunbog, sir, have you ever been there?"

Mr. Lunbog! Another stroke of fright. This man was the factor, the very man Fitzhugh had come to see in Annapolis. And would see. In short, between Mr. Sandys and this Mr. Lunbog, I was caught in the very catastrophe that Bara had warned me might occur.

I was too confounded to move.

"Go there?" returned Mr. Lunbog, and he puffed upon his pipe so that smoke wreathed his face, suggesting a fat angel looking out from a heavenly cloud. "But why?" he said to me. "Is not our beloved Annapolis fair enough?"

The slowness of Mr. Lunbog's speech agitated me. "Please, sir," I felt myself obliged to say, "I was asked to find out where Philadelphia is; near or far?"

"Come now. What gentleman would ask you to find out such a thing in this place and time of night?"

Though no quick lie came to mind, I was too panicky to move away from the peril into which I had placed myself.

The big man actually laughed, which set his heavy cheeks as well as his whole belly into jovial motion. Then he drew deeply on his pipe and let the tobacco smoke seep slowly through his ruddy lips.

"Now then, my boy," he continued, "I am obliged to inquire: Have you the required written permission to come here and ask such a question? Are you on a legitimate errand for your master?"

"Le-legitimate, sir?" I stammered, and struggled to put on my most innocent face, while working hard not to look at Mr. Sandys.

"Come, come, Mr. Sandys," said the big man. "Advise me: Are my eyes not performing properly in this muggy gloom? Is this boy not wearing a convict collar?"

In my mad haste, I had forgotten I had the iron round my neck. My terror increased.

Sandys only said, "I have larger news."

"Larger news?" said the big man. "Pray, who is this news for?"

"This boy," said Sandys.

Mr. Lunbog looked from me to Mr. Sandys and back again. "Do you mean to say, sir, you actually know this boy?"

"We have a mutual friend. Or had one. In England."

"Now that, sir," proclaimed the big man, "is truly

remarkable. Here we are in Maryland, but you two share a friend in distant England. I could not have imagined it. Would you elucidate this for me, sir?"

I could only gawk at Sandys, fearful that he was about to say something that would do me great harm.

What he said was: "It regards Mr. Jonathan Wild."

Surely, the last words I expected.

The big man puffed his pipe placidly. "Begad, sir," said Lunbog. "I know that name. England's chief villain. The most despicable, sir, I have ever heard. Yet, you say that not only do you know this boy but you share a connection to that rogue. What could this boy have to do with the infamous Mr. Wild?"

Sandys looked at me and smiled. "You might like to know, Master Pitts, word has come since I saw you last. In London, not long ago, Mr. Wild was arrested, convicted, taken to the triple tree at Tyburn, and hanged. Tickets were sold to witness the event. Thousands came to see it happen and cheer the scoundrel off."

Frozen, I hardly knew how to respond.

"Did I hear you say this boy's name?" said Lunbog to Sandys. "I must repeat my question. What might he have to do with Wild? Is that why he wears the iron collar?"

"Ask him," said Sandys, a grin upon his face.

Lunbog turned to me. "Boy, I'd truly like to know.

Were you on familiar terms with Mr. Wild?" He put a plump hand to his heart. "I am an honest fellow, but thieves have a sharpness I admire."

Not knowing what else to say, I fairly cried, "Please, sir, I . . . I just want to know about Philadelphia. Where is it?"

At which point Sandys laughed as if I had said something very funny.

"To answer your question," said Lunbog. "Philadelphia is a city. A large one, I've been informed, though I never saw the place. It's in Pennsylvania colony. To the northeast of us, a hundred and twenty odd miles. As for getting there, I cannot imagine the roads would be good, if they exist at all. No, best go by water, north upon the bay.

"But, my dear boy," the big man went on, "be forewarned, Pennsylvania is a country full of Quakers. Odd folk. They won't swear allegiance to the Crown. But I must ask: Why desire to go there?"

I was not about to say. In any case, I'd learned what I wished to know—that Philadelphia was north and east, not far. Wanting to do nothing but leave, I shifted my feet, ready to dash off.

"Stay put," cried Lunbog, and I, having become so habituated to taking orders, did exactly that.

"Let us speak plainly, my dear boy, which is my preference. You"—he leveled a thick finger at me—"young as you are, must be a transported convict. Your iron collar tells me so. Your history"—he glanced at Sandys—"suggests as much."

I was incapable of doing anything but stand there.

"Are you aware," Lunbog continued loudly, "that according to Maryland law, I could be awarded two hundred true pounds of tobacco for simply apprehending you? Two hundred blessed pounds.

"Now, boy," he went on, "would that not be a fine profit for my pocket for just sitting here of a hot summer eve, taking my pipe while conversing with a friend? All I need do is tell this man"—he gestured to Sandys—"in his capacity, dare I say it, his obligation, as town watchman, to apprehend you, and I would become richer." He laughed again. "What have you to say to that?"

Too confounded to speak I remained mute.

Sandys, however, leaned in. "Well sir," he said to Lunbog, "without going into the particulars, which would be demeaning to all, I feel I have some responsibility for this boy. I suspect he's unfortunate in his condition. As I once was. He served me then. I should do so for him now. Let me urge you to let the boy go—with a warning."

"What warning?"

"That if I ever saw him making so free again, I would be obliged to apprehend him."

"Mr. Sandys, sir, I shall take your plea into my large

heart. Now, then, dear boy, we shall rejoice in Mr. Sandys's kindness by not detaining you. Be off. But heed the watchman's words: don't ever let us see you again."

Feeling great relief, I was just about to run off when the big man added, "Hold!"

I stopped.

"You brought a dark friend with you, did you not?" said Mr. Lunbog in his loudest voice.

In the instant, I knew he was referring to Bara. But how?

"He is standing some ways back, right there, wishing not to be seen. He goes by the name of Bara. Am I not correct?"

Lunbog pointed farther up along the wharf. "You might inform him I saw him. I know him. Warn him. I know his master, the unpleasant Mr. Fitzhugh." Mr. Lunbog guffawed as if it was all a great joke. "Now flee, boy. Dash away."

Appalled and altogether unnerved, I bolted off, though how I ran on my wobbly legs I cannot say. Bara, I realized, not only had followed me, no doubt trying to restrain me, but had been seen. It was the very thing he had warned me might happen. My only thought was to get back to him and give warning. But when I reached the spot where Lunbog had seen him, he was not there.

CHAPTER FORTY-SEVEN

In Which I Am Lost.

Bara gone.

As I grasped that what I'd done put us in grave danger, it's impossible to say which sensation—fear, confusion, or mortification—tangled me more. In truth, my legs felt boneless. "Stupid, stupid, stupid," I said to myself. Fearful that Bara had left me in anger, I kept turning circles, trying to find him. That included looking where I could still observe Mr. Sandys and Mr. Lunbog sitting on the wharf. The big man's glowing pipe was stirring about. Was he watching to see what I was doing? Where I had gone? Where Bara was?

There came a great *crack* as lightning burst from the sky. In my distressed state, the explosion caused me to wince. That bolt was followed by a rolling rattle of thunder that unnerved me even more. Rain began to pour. In an instant, I was soaked.

More than wet, I was confounded. Bara, the one I needed, wanted, was nowhere in sight. Moreover, in the cascading rain, I was utterly muddled. Not knowing what to do I did nothing but remain in place.

Given this painful reminder as to how dependent I was on Bara, the best I could speculate was that he had gone back to the Royal George, the tavern from where we had started. Accordingly, from doing nothing, I began to race up the street, going back the way I had come.

Whether to guide or mock me, lightning continued to explode, thunder cannoned, and rain streamed. Half blind, utterly distracted, I splattered through the muddy streets, going breakneck along a narrow way from which several small streets led. I had barely passed one of these small lanes when I was abruptly snatched from behind by a powerful grip while a hand covered my mouth. Prevented from crying out, I was dragged into the side way and spun about.

It was Bara who had taken hold of me. Hardly knowing whether I was relieved or abashed, I said, "I'm sor—"

"You idiot," Bara shouted into my face as the rain showered us. When more lightning exploded, I thought I saw tears coursing down his face. His anguish was awful to witness.

"I heard him," cried Bara. "That factor—Lunbog saw me. He knows me and my connection to Fitzhugh. He's the person the old man came to town to see. And that other man, the watchman, he recognized you. You heard him."

"But, surely, he won't—"

"You don't know anything about what Lunbog will or won't do," cried Bara, his anger building.

"But . . . but I have to find my sister," I said.

"Forget your sister," shouted Bara with a fury such as I had never heard from him. "I'm trying to save my life."

That time I could have no doubt: I did see tears.

Horrified by the consequence of my folly, filled with shame, I knew not what to say.

"Lunbog loves the sound of his own voice," Bara went on. "If the only thing that stood by him was a stone he'd gossip to it. Do you think he won't tell Fitzhugh that we were on the wharf without permission? And you asking about that Philadelphia? When the old man learns of it, what do you think he'll do?"

When I didn't, couldn't answer, Bara reached out, gripped me by both shoulders, and shook me hard. "Think, Oliver," he shouted into my face. "He'll do to us what he did to Clark: murder us."

My stupidity could not be stated more clearly.

But Bara wasn't finished. "You were only going after what you wished to know. You gave no thought to me."

"I'm . . . I'm sorry," I struggled to get out. "I truly am. I just wanted to—"

"Use your wits, Oliver. The moment the old man discovers what we were about—what you said and did—he'll be after us with double wrath. And I'd been waiting, planning for the right time to run off."

"I didn't think."

"Oliver," Bara cried with exasperation. "You've made my plans useless. Fitzhugh won't wait on us. If we want to live, we must get away. Now."

"But how? Where?"

"There's only one way: the swamp."

"The swamp?" I echoed lamely. What I wanted to say is that I had no more chance of surviving there than would a butterfly's shadow. All I said, however, was, "But . . . but the swamp is . . . is far north."

"Which means we have to get there before Fitzhugh overtakes us. Tonight."

The rain was coming down with increasing force.

"I'll tell you true," said Bara in a voice painfully hard for me to hear, "I'm not sure I want you to come with me. Not if you're so dull. You either do as I say, or you can find your own way."

"No, please," I pleaded. "I won't be thoughtless again. I can't run away without you."

Bara stared at me. "Do what you want," he said. "I'm leaving." He shoved me aside, burst out of the alley onto the bigger street, and began to run.

I rushed out and caught up to him. "Forgive me," I called out again. "Please. I'll do what you say. Let me go with you."

Bara did not even deign to look at me. "To begin, put your sister out of your mind. No talk of finding her. We need to save ourselves. That's the only thing that matters. If you can't stay with me, I'll go alone. Will you understand that?"

"Yes."

"Now, no chatter. Just move."

Bara, his back to me, ran as fast as he could beneath the sluicing rain. I, with less leg, struggled to keep up.

We passed through town, whose streets had turned into rivers of mud. Then the rain eased and stopped as quickly as it had come. The moon returned and offered some light. When we drew near the Royal George, I whispered, "Can't we take his horse?"

"No," Bara snapped. "He's sleeping right by it. It might wake him. Besides, a horse is useless in the swamp. But there's something we must have at the plantation."

It was hardly the time to ask what he meant. Instead, we went round the tavern with utmost caution, lest we somehow wake Fitzhugh. Then it wasn't long before we were on the dirt track heading north, beyond Annapolis, going as fast as we could, me struggling to keep up with Bara.

We were running north to save ourselves, to gain our freedom, but, I tell it true, we were going to a place—the swamp—that I truly dreaded. I tried not to think of that. With fear snapping at my heels, in the moment, my sole desire was to stay with Bara.

CHAPTER FORTY-EIGHT

The Ever-shifting Dark.

B y my reckoning, it was the third time I had passed
along that road, but those other times were during
daylight. This time it was dark, though moonlight came
and went, oft times hidden by streaks of swiftly moving
clouds. The deserted way we followed was like an endless
tunnel, forward and behind. Trees walled us in on either
side, so that a looming vagueness prevailed, no matter
where we looked. It meant while our desire was to go fast,
the reality was otherwise. We had to find our way, until
our eyes grew weary of always staring hard into nothing,
always fearful of seeing something.

Far away, lightning flashed followed by thunder, which
echoed my thudding heart. The ever-changing light, when
it came, kept altering the look of the road, so it was as if
I had never traveled the route before. Though we did not

talk, the *slap, slap* of our bare feet upon the muddy road was like handclaps in a vast and empty hall.

My fear that we might be apprehended at any moment helped me ignore the ache in my side and the spikes of pain when my bare feet struck stones along the way. I just ran, full of a deep sense of fault, thinking what I might do to make amends to Bara.

Looming over all else was our constant dread that we would be overtaken by Fitzhugh. To be sure, I wanted to believe the old man was far behind, sleeping off his drunken stupor. But he had instilled so deep a fear in me, I was equally willing to believe he had powers that allowed him to know we were fleeing, and where we were. Thus, as I peered into the shadows before us, I continually looked back over my shoulder into still more shadows.

Then we reached the river.

It was the same over which we had passed with ease by ferry. Now it lay before us, a broad, deep band of darkness. As much as we could see it, we heard it tumbling by. Even in the sodden gloom we could see rain had given it high volume. It flickered with white flecks of moonlight, as if stars had fallen, only to be swept away by the force of the water.

To my eyes, the distance across appeared greater than I recalled. My heart squeezed; crossing to the other side seemed impossible. Once again came that phrase: "He who is born to be drowned will never be hanged." But standing there, much alarmed, I reversed it: "He who was never hanged is born to be drowned."

I could just see the river's far side, and the small house where the ferryman—that Mr. Eps—most likely lived. Presumably he was there since his flat-bottom boat rested on that side. Since no light came from his dwelling, hopefully he slept. But what if he woke? I recalled how big and powerful he was.

As for the rope, which Mr. Eps used to haul his craft from one side to the other, it was in place, to my eyes, hardly thicker than a spider's thread.

Bara picked up a bit of branch and threw it into the river. The powerful flow whisked it away.

"We need to get over," Bara said. He was speaking the obvious, but I knew he was telling me I had no choice.

While I remained unnerved, Bara walked straight into the river, where frothing white water curled about his legs. He wrapped his arms around himself, which told me it was cold, too.

He took another step deeper and looked around. I had not moved. "Are you coming?"

"I can't swim."

Bara said nothing, only offering what I took to be an exasperated look.

I called, "I'll go upriver until it gets shallow."

"We can't take the time." He moved farther into the river, reminding me of the urgency. I could have no doubt: if I did not cross over he would leave me behind.

I glanced up at the rope that stretched across the river. "I'll use this," I called. So he would know I was in earnest. I went to the pole where the rope was affixed.

The rope was above my head, but not by so very much. I glanced at Bara. He had moved along so that the water was up to his waist. My choice was obvious: Remain on this side of the river and lose Bara as well as my life, or try to cross the river and *perhaps* lose my life. I chose perhaps.

I leaped up, grasped the rope with my right hand, and then with my left—one hand behind the other—so that I was now dangling above the land, sideways to the river. I clenched the rope so forcefully my fingers hurt. My hanging weight made my arms ache as well. I shifted one hand from back to front—then the other—thereby drawing myself forward along the rope while dangling over the water.

Meanwhile, Bara had plunged into the water and began to kick and waggle his arms and legs, rather like a horse or dog might do—his head up. I grasped that he was swimming—an action I'd rarely seen before by humans. It allowed him to make progress getting across.

That goaded me. Working as fast as I could, I continued to move hand over hand, out over the river. The rope sagged with my weight so my toes were inches above the water.

As I moved along, the rope swayed and bounced, which meant at times my feet went into the river. My fingers burned from the rope, and my arms, which held all my weight, gave increasing pain. Nonetheless, I inched along.

At mid-river, I gave myself a pause and took a deep breath, telling myself I could go the rest of the way.

I pressed on, shifting hands as before, one before the other, making slow but certain headway. I tried to keep my eyes from the water, but instead watched Bara, following him, since he remained in front of me, still swimming. He was already near the river's other side.

Going farther, my arms began to pain me more. Then my left arm and hand suddenly turned rigid with a cramp, unbearably painful, making it impossible to flex my fingers.

To give myself some relief, I forced myself to release my left-hand grip, so that I was now dangling solely by my right hand while I tried to shake out that left-hand cramp.

But that one hand could not hold. Instead, I fell.

CHAPTER FORTY-NINE

In the River.

I plunged straight into the water, my head going under. Frantic, knowing I would drown, the best I could do was to thrash my arms, seeking to climb up and claim some air. Instead, I only swallowed a throatful of water.

Gagging, I sank anew.

My arms flailed, my legs kicked. Somehow I went up, only to go down, then up again, my head full of roaring sounds. But that time when I went under and deeper, my toe struck something firm. My chest squeezed.

Desperate, I shoved my other foot down and found— to my vast relief—support. It was, I hoped, the river bottom or at least a rock. With urgent effort, I managed to stand, bursting upward so I was able to extend my head— stretching my neck up, head tilted back—until my chin barely crested above the river. It was enough.

Coughing, choking, sputtering, I spat my mouth free of water, struggled for breath, and stood in place, shivering with cold and fright.

It took some moments to clear my thoughts, my eyes, my lungs, and calm my pounding heart. When I was finally able to see through blurry eyes where I was, the opposite riverbank appeared not so far away. Dashing through the water toward me was Bara, hand extended.

I lunged at his hand, grasped it, and though I could stand on my feet, more than anything, was dragged to the shore. Once there I collapsed on the land. With Bara standing over me, I pulled my knees into my chest, coughed repeatedly, and worked to regain my gasping breath.

"I thought you were gone," said Bara.

I nodded. "I owe . . . you my life," I managed to say.

"No," he said, "you owe me mine. We must keep going." He reached down. I grasped his hand and he helped me regain my feet. He poked my shoulder. "You'll be all right." Then he added, "Will you?"

Dripping wet, legs unsteady, I nodded.

Side by side, with me still weak and shivering from the scare, the two of us went up to the slight embankment, slipped silently past the ferryman's dark house, and regained the road.

As we entered onto that shadowy path, I shuddered and glanced back at the river to see the danger I had just avoided. On the far bank, looking like a wrathful spirit in the moonlight, a horse and rider galloped down to the river's edge.

"Bara," I whispered, and pulled him around.

Bara looked. "Him," he said. I didn't need to be told whom he meant: Fitzhugh.

Whether the old man saw us or not, we didn't stay to learn. We turned and tore along the road, now and again pausing to peer back, listening so as to learn if he was still coming.

It wasn't long before we heard a gunshot. I looked to Bara.

"He's calling the ferryman to get him across."

We raced on.

Not long after, Bara cried, "Into the trees!" He plunged into the thickets, where he threw himself down. I did the same.

A horse came galloping by. It was as if the thunder had followed us. As hooves pounded past in the direction we were heading, we pressed our faces to the ground and dared not move until the sounds faded to nothing.

We pushed ourselves up, crept back to the road, and peered where the horse had gone.

There we were, hardly more than two scared boys, standing side by side in our scraggy clothing and bare feet, on that empty, moonlit, muddy road. The air was moist and sticky, the light just enough so that I could see the fear on Bara's face, which I have no doubt must have been what was on mine. I listened but heard no sound save chirping crickets.

Though I already knew the answer to the question, I said, my voice low but filled with fear, "Was that *him?*"

"Think so."

"Was he going home?"

"Probably."

"When he doesn't find us there, will he come back along the road?"

Bara did not reply, but stood, staring north. "He might," he said. "He's not a man who usually gallops. I can tell one thing for sure: He's in a rage. Which means when he doesn't find us there, he'll get others to help catch us. We're runaways now. If they take us, we won't be going anywhere else. Ever."

Thinking of Clark, and recalling all too vividly the grave in which he lay, I waited for Bara to tell me what to do. When he remained silent, I considered: Should we go back to town, where Lunbog and Sandys might catch us? Or forward, where Fitzhugh would try to do the same? It appeared to make no difference. Neither seemed the right answer.

I said, "I'm sorry I went to the wharf."

Bara didn't even look at me. "It's done. We're here."

I said nothing.

At last Bara spoke. "He'll be thinking we're going toward home."

"Why?"

"Told you: The only way I know how to get free and away is through the swamp. He'd know that."

At that moment, I wasn't about to share my fear of the swamp.

He went on: "Just hope the rain didn't go there. The swamp will fill. Make it harder to pass through."

That agitated me further, but I remained mute.

Bara must have guessed my thoughts. "Oliver, it's the only safe place. Trouble is, I'm not certain where it spreads. I just know two sure things. It starts up there and then goes west. I know the way in—first part anyway. We have to reach the maroons." He stood still for a moment. Then he said, "We need a knife."

"Why?" I had to ask again.

"No saying what we'll meet up with as we go through. Bears. Cougars. Or Fitzhugh."

"Where you going to get a knife?"

"Hog pen."

He said nothing more, a reminder of his earlier warnings about knowing nothing that Fitzhugh might beat out of me.

"Right now," he said, "we need to move as best we

can. Keep listening. Watching. Be ready to bolt. You have better ideas?"

I shook my head.

"Another thing. You might not want to hear it."

"What?"

"It'll be a whole lot better if we go together. But I can't keep taking care of you. You need to stop asking me if the sun is going to rise in the morning. We're past that."

"I understand," I said. Still, I felt the rebuke and judged him to be right.

Then he added, "You need to know something else."

I waited.

"I wouldn't do this unless I thought you could."

"I will," I said, grateful and strengthened by his words. "I will."

We started again. This time, however, instead of going away from Fitzhugh, we were running toward him.

CHAPTER FIFTY

In Which We Travel Deeper into Darkness.

From that time on, rather than running, we walked fast so as to reserve our strength. As much effort went into listening and watching. Any number of times, Bara called "Stop." Then we'd both halt and strain our ears, our eyes. Though we never saw or heard anyone, fear populates darkness. Not for a moment did I feel safe.

All that night we traveled along an empty road. Without moonlight, I don't know what we would have done. Fortunate, too, that Bara had passed this way a goodly number of times. Thus, he led and I was content to follow, and we both refrained from speaking.

We reached another river and to my silent disappointment, no rope was there. Though this river was not as big as the previous one, it was rain-swollen and flowing swiftly.

As I hesitated on the shore, Bara waded right in. He did not even look back to see if I was following. Despite my unease, after a few steps, I was up to my waist. I pushed on and by mid-river water reached my chest.

I had little choice but to press forward, determined to show Bara I could be strong. Heart thumping, I held my breath, clamped my mouth shut, and flung myself forward. No sooner did my feet come off the river bottom than I began to be swept away. Fearful I'd sink like a stone, I imitated what Bara had done, his kind of swimming: thrashing my arms, kicking legs, which to my elation was sufficient to carry me through the few feet I was unable to walk.

"Now I don't have to teach you to swim," said Bara as I stumbled upon the other shore, where he was waiting. It was as much a relief to have him praise me, and see him smile, as it was to reach land.

We continued on. As we drew nearer to Fitzhugh's land, I began to notice a change in Bara. I sensed his excitement and urgency and took strength from it, telling myself it wasn't fright.

"What do we do when we get to the farm?"

"First thing: see if he's there or not."

"Think he will be?"

"Hope not."

"You glad we're going to run away?"

"It wasn't my plan to go like this. It is now."

We passed over more small streams, which required me to swim again but, in my way, I had learned the art.

A red dawn began to show to the east between trees. The light on the road turned gray.

Bara halted. "We need to hide. It'll be safer to get there at night." He led the way among trees.

We spent the whole day concealed, waiting for the darkness to return. The insects swarmed about us, on us. My stomach churned with hunger, as did Bara's. We had not eaten for a whole day. Sometimes Bara slept, and I watched. Then I slept and found some relief while he watched.

It was a long day. At one point, there was another heavy fall of rain, and we could only endure it. Happily, it did not last long, but I had visions of the swamp water rising ever higher. The more I tried not to think about that, the more I did.

Now and again walkers, riders on horses, or wagons passed along the road. Some moved quickly as if in pursuit. Each time someone went by, we hugged the ground and dared not to look up. If they were looking for us—Fitzhugh might have even been among them—we could gain no intelligence.

Night returned, and once again we set out upon the road, walking north. Clouds had lifted. The rain had ceased. The moon was bright. The air heavy with summer heat. Knowing we were drawing ever closer, and fearful of what we'd find, we didn't speak. It was still dark when we finally came to the edge of Fitzhugh's plantation.

CHAPTER FIFTY-ONE

The Knife.

We stood on the verge of the woods and stared down over Fitzhugh's land. The nighttime summer heat pressed on my face like a hot, damp, and heavy hand. Moonlight painted all with a pale, yellowy hue save the shadows, which were blacker than the dark. The old man's house was dark, too, offering no hint if he was there or not. Yet everything about the place reminded me of his evil. There was nothing that was not him. Even the dense tobacco fields, with their tall stalks and huge leaves, were full of threat. What sounds there were came from the whirring of invisible insects and chirping crickets, like the ticking of a hurried clock.

From somewhere behind us came a low-pitched roar. It made me start, but though I listened hard, the sound didn't repeat itself.

"Bear," Bara whispered.

"Is that why we have to get the knife?"

"I told you what might be there. Besides, if Fitzhugh comes after us . . ."

I stared down over the land. "Doesn't look like he's here. Maybe when he didn't find us on the road, he went back to town to look for us. Maybe we're safe."

Bara said, "And maybe he wants us to think he isn't here. It would fit his fancy to take us by surprise."

"That knife's in the hog pen, isn't it?" I finally asked.

"Where I put it," said Bara.

"Do you think . . . he might know?"

"Hope not."

"That's what you did the other night, isn't it? When he was deep drunk: you went down and took it."

"Uh-huh."

"Did you . . . did you think of killing him?"

He nodded. "Course I did. But if it had gone wrong, he'd have killed me right then. I don't care a kernel of corn about his life. I just want mine. You ever hear people say, 'When I die I hope I'll go to Heaven'?"

"Yes."

"Well, if I can have my freedom, that'll be Heaven enough for me."

We continued to remain in place. Bara was still staring over the land. I was sure he was searching for Fitzhugh and was as uneasy as I was. That helped me, because Bara's fear told me my fear was sensible.

Making a show of bravery out of my dread of being left alone, I said, "We can get the knife together. You always said those hogs were vicious."

"They eat anything, even people. I put the knife there hoping they'd protect it. Now I'm hoping they don't."

He took a deep breath, as if to prepare himself. Without saying more, he started off along the path that separated the tobacco fields, walking with care, footsteps soft. I kept close, alert for the smallest hint of Fitzhugh. At the bottom of the slope the bay shimmered under the bright moonlight. I started at the sound of a distant splash but told myself it was nothing more than a jumping fish.

"Couldn't we get away by that canoe?" I whispered.

"He keeps the paddle in his chest," Bara reminded me.

Some twenty feet from the stables we heard the sound of a horse whicker. That stopped us dead.

"His horse," Bara whispered.

I knew what that meant: Fitzhugh was about.

CHAPTER FIFTY-TWO

The Hog Pen.

H eart hammering, I wanted to say, "Let's leave the knife behind," but didn't dare.

Bara resumed moving toward the pen. He reached its gate. The hogs snuffled and grunted at his arrival. With great care, Bara lifted the pen latch. I set myself behind him, searching over the land so if Fitzhugh showed himself I might see. If he caught us by surprise we'd be trapped.

The gate scraped open.

I heard something moving in the pen, which spun me around. The largest hog had lumbered to his feet. He was enormous. As if food were about to be delivered, the beast was looking right at Bara. Its wet snout dripping, the hog offered up a deep, throaty grunt. Whether it was a welcome or a warning I could not tell.

Bara took a step toward the feed box. With alarming

speed, the hog shambled forward and placed his huge self between the feed box and Bara. He lifted his heavy head. From his raw, open mouth, spittle drooled and I could see his ragged teeth. His eyes were glossy.

Bara looked to me in appeal.

I ran into the pen. "Where's the knife?"

"In the corn."

I darted round the hog to the corn box and looked within. It was full of cobs. Using both hands to search for the knife, I simultaneously shoveled the corn out onto the ground, tossing it as far as I could. That was enough for the hogs. The big one lumbered over and began to root among the feed. The other hogs, squealing and grunting, joined him in an eating frenzy.

Seeing his way clear, Bara jumped to the food box and plunged his hands deep in, emptying it, looking for the knife.

I backed off. One of the hogs, thinking I meant to steal his food, lunged at my leg. I scrambled away and retreated into a corner of the pen, as far from Bara as possible. The beast advanced, head low, never taking his glinting eyes from me. He pawed the ground and grunted. His upper lip pulled back, showing his teeth.

"Got it," I heard. I looked up. Bara was holding up the blade.

The hog that had been advancing on me turned in

the direction of Bara's voice, saw the other pigs with their snouts in the corn, and lumbered away to eat with the others.

With the pigs uninterested in us, Bara and I darted out of the pen, not bothering to latch it shut.

Even as we did, we heard the loud report of a gun.

That stopped us hard.

It was clear: not only did Fitzhugh know we were there, he wanted us to know it.

CHAPTER FIFTY-THREE

In Which We Flee for Our Lives.

D o . . . do you see him?" I said, my voice choked.
"No," said Bara as he looked all ways around.
"But he knows where we are. He'll want to torment us
before he kills us."

To my surprise, Bara, the knife gripped in his hand,
began to run up the slope. I scrambled to stay with him.
To our right and left were tobacco fields. The goal became
obvious: the swamp. Get there and—if Fitzhugh didn't
catch us—we'd be free.

But we hadn't gone very far when we saw the old man.
Blocking our escape, he was standing at the crest of the
hill, illuminated by a flaming torch. There could be no
doubt he fully intended us to see him and the musket
that was in his other hand. It was deeply unnerving. Let

no one tell you that the Devil isn't smart. He's also full of vanity.

"I trust you see me," Fitzhugh cried. I heard glee in his voice.

"Now then," he called down to where we stood frozen, "whichever one of you takes hold of the other and brings him to me, I'll spare. I don't care which of you does it. I just want one. Don't doubt me; I'm willing to kill you both and pleased to replace you. Trash like you comes cheap and easy."

We didn't move.

"Make up your minds," shouted Fitzhugh. "Who wishes to live? Be quick now."

To give strength to his threat, he pushed the sharp point of his torch handle into the ground, wherein it stuck and flamed like his own private sun. Thus illuminated, and both hands free, he lifted his musket and leveled it at us—but at which one, we could not know.

Bara and I stood where we were gawping with indecision. Meanwhile, the old man remained before us with the clear intent of murdering at least one.

Then I felt Bara's foot touch mine. Since we were standing side by side, he could not have moved it more than an inch. Perhaps less. All the same, in that tiny touch, I knew Bara's thoughts as certain as if he had shouted into my ear: He would not give me up. And when I returned the gesture, I was telling him I would not give him up.

Let it be said, one touch, however small, can convey volumes. What Bara told me with that touch and what I told him in turn: that we would stand—or fall—as one. I tell you true, I felt a surge of strength and resolution.

Fitzhugh still had his gun leveled at us.

I heard Bara say, "Run."

That word—"run"—might have been small, yet Bara was no more than halfway through it when he burst away, me sprinting by his side, heading straight toward a field of tobacco plants.

Fitzhugh fired his musket. The musket ball whipped by, followed almost instantly by the *bang*. I felt no pain and heard nothing from Bara to tell me he had been struck. Our quick movements had allowed us to evade his first shot.

We plunged directly among the tobacco plants, which at that late season were tall, taller for the most part than me and a fair number taller than Bara. He slashed frantically with the knife to cut them down. We would not have gotten through otherwise. Nor forget it was still night, and the tobacco plants, with their large leaves, made everything that much more obscure. It was as if the shadows had taken on solidity. Moreover, as we ran, we had to be stooped so as to remain poor targets. Nor did I have any idea which direction to go, but moved in Bara's wake as fast as possible.

Behind us came the crashing, crushing sounds of the old man in frenetical pursuit. To make matters worse it was we who were opening a wide path that he could follow with far greater ease. He also had his burning torch to show him our path.

Another *bang*. Another musket ball flew past.

We burst out at the far side of the field, and while our way was no longer restricted, we were now exposed. If anything, Bara ran harder. I did, too. Once, twice, I glanced back to see if we were being pursued. Sure enough, Fitzhugh was following, still brandishing his flame though not gaining on us. But then he halted, and with a violent curse, flung the torch forward, so that its fire arched through the air, a blazing star, only to drop and lie upon the ground, still burning.

While it did not reach us, it was sufficiently close that I could have no doubt it illuminated us more, making for a clearer target. Sure enough, Fitzhugh paused and worked to reload his gun.

That's when Bara spun about and ran back—in Fitzhugh's direction. Astonished by what he was doing, I could only stand mazed and watch.

On the run, Bara reached the flaming torch, picked it

up by its handle, and flung it back so that it landed behind Fitzhugh, midst the tobacco plants. Almost immediately I saw a lick of flame leap up.

Fitzhugh must have seen it too. He spun about to face the tobacco field.

As Bara ran back toward me, the fire spread quickly through the dry tobacco as new flares shot up and spread. The pop and snap of burning filled my ears. The heavy sot-weed stench was rank. The billowing smoke, illuminated by fire, became a swirling, scarlet cloud. In a matter of seconds the whole tobacco field was engulfed in flames. Even from where we stood I could feel the heat.

Stunned, Bara and I watched.

We saw Fitzhugh, as if shocked, move toward the flames, perhaps believing he could stop it.

We did not wait to see more, but plunged back into a different tobacco field. As Bara cut more plants, I pushed them away. Not until we reached the far side of that field did we stop again and, with lungs heaving for breath, peer back.

No sign of Fitzhugh. What we did see was that the flames now covered a large expanse of land, with whole fields engulfed by fire. I had no doubt Fitzhugh was the Devil. Now, to match, his farm was a burning hell.

Bara broke my trance by pulling at me. "The swamp," he said with great urgency.

We ran again. It wasn't long before I sensed the ground beneath my feet grow soft, telling me we were approaching the swamp. In my mind, it loomed before us as nothing, a black hole in the equally black night.

My courage and strength faltered. I used the sharp pain in my side as an excuse to stop running.

Bara, breathing hard, stopped beside me. We both looked back to the flames, higher and wider than ever.

"If he's trapped in there," I said, "we might already be free."

It was my last defense against going into the swamp.

"Or he might still be coming after us," Bara said. "We need to hurry."

Even as he spoke, he vanished into the forward darkness, toward the swamp.

Let it be admitted, even then I hesitated. As far as I was concerned, I had been carried by the *Owners Goodwill* to the end of the world. Now I was being asked to go beyond.

I cannot tell you how long I stood there, caught as it were between two horrors. Then ahead, out of the dark, I heard Bara call, "You coming?"

Not wanting to be left behind, I dashed on, even as

the ground kept getting softer. In short order, I began to splash through water. That was when I realized I had stopped going forward. Instead, I was sinking into mud, unable to move.

CHAPTER FIFTY-FOUR

The Swamp.

My left leg was clagged in mire, which gripped with giant strength and, like some living thing, refused to let me go. If I moved, it sucked me deeper so that even as I sank down, my terror rose. Desperate, I looked for Bara only to see darkness, darkness below, darkness above, darkness everywhere. Around me, the swamp gurgled while unseen insects fluskered against my face like tiny fingers.

I tried to free myself by thrusting my right foot down only to have that leg held just as tightly. The best I could manage was to twist and turn, but to my further alarm, those movements caused me to lose all sense of direction—and worse, pulled me that much deeper.

"Bara," I screamed. "I'm caught. I can't move. Where are you?"

"Here."

Somewhere close, but in all that engulfing darkness I couldn't see him, not a hint.

"Where are you?" I heard him cry.

"Here. Caught in mud," I yelled, and tried again to pull myself free, only to slip deeper. "Hurry. I'm sinking."

"Keep talking," he said. "I'm coming."

"Here," I cried. "Here."

Though Bara was invisible, sounds of his splashing steps drew near. For my part I stretched out my arms—waving them about in all directions, trying to reach him. All I grabbed was nothing. Then, as I swung my hands about in the darkness, I felt his fingers, as he must have felt mine. He grabbed me.

"Got you," he said.

"Pull," I pleaded.

His hands shifted and gripped my wrist. He had me now—as I had him—four hands joined. As he began to back up, I began to rise slowly out of the mud.

"Keep holding on," he instructed, but the reality was, he was holding me.

Every inch required effort. Each step took strength. All of this struggle took place in the dark; I could not see him—or anything else for that matter. Still, we labored until I felt firmness beneath my knees, reaching solid earth.

With great effort, I yanked my right foot free. Then my left. Released, I stumbled forward.

"Keep coming," Bara urged.

I moved forward—walking on my knees.

Sopping wet, my body garbed in clinging mud, I managed to stand. Bara's hand steadied me. Gasping for breath, I stared about, but I cannot say I understood where I was. I could see nothing, no stars, no moon, just blackness.

"Where . . . are we?" I said.

"Not sure."

I turned in the direction from which I believed we'd come. I thought I saw a flickering of flames at some distance, which I took to be Fitzhugh's tobacco fields.

"Still burning," I said.

"Looks it."

"Do you think he's alive?"

"If he is, he'll be coming after us. And not just him."

I leaned over and touched about the solid ground, finding grasses and bushes. To the best of my senses, it appeared as if we were on an isle of earth, but whether small or great, I could not tell. Spent, I sat down.

Bara sat close by.

"If you hadn't come, I would have disappeared," I said.

"But you didn't." Then he said, "It's a good thing you're my younger brother."

"Why?" I said, pleased he called me "brother."

"Because if you were older you'd have no excuses."

A small jest but it calmed me. I allowed myself a deep breath. "How many times have you saved me?"

"Too many. But you saved me from those hogs. You were with me in the fire."

"No more than that?"

"You need not worry. We have a long way to go."

I looked into the darkness. "Is the whole swamp like this?" I asked.

"I was told there are many small, solid islands. They're here, there. Can you see now why I didn't want to go alone? What happened to you could—will—happen to me. You'll save me then."

"The ones who told you about the maroons, did they say where you would find them?"

"Miles west. It's all secret."

I reached for my pocket only to find it torn. Moreover, Charity's lace bit was gone. It was as if I were struck in the chest. And here I was in the swamp moving away from her, with no idea if I would ever reach that Philadelphia. I said nothing to Bara. What could I say? Though I told myself I should be content to breathe, it couldn't feel that way.

Bara stood up. "We need to keep going."

I gazed into the darkness. "Now?" I asked.

"Be better by day. But—"

"But what?"

"Day will mean we can see better but the other way is true, too: we'll be a lot easier to see."

I continued to sit. "How are we to go?"

"Remember the skipping stone?"

"I suppose."

"Same as that. We'll skip from one isle to another."

I gazed into the dark swamp. I could see very little. "How long will it take?" I said.

"Not sure it matters."

"Why?"

"Oliver, I'll say it once and not again; we've got but one chance. Because we can't go back, can we?"

Knowing he was right, I looked but could no longer see the fire. Instead, I turned and faced the darkness. The darkness would be all the light we had.

CHAPTER FIFTY-FIVE

In Which We Move through the Swamp, Where a Frightful Thing Happens.

It took no time for us to cross to the far side of the little island, after which we returned into the swamp waters, the level coming up to my waist. It sent a scissoring chill through me, but not so much from its temperature, as from dread.

We began to walk. Impossible to say who led, who followed, or even where we went. Often, to reassure myself, I reached out and touched Bara. He did the same to me. We exchanged no talk, save muffled reassurances passing back and forth. The loudest noises were the soft, steady plashing water and the constant chirr of insects. Our splashing must have kept the snakes and animals at bay—at least I never heard them.

As we pressed on, the water was sometimes low,

sometimes high, always slimy underfoot, one place firm, another soft. Thus we stumbled on, bumping into logs, roots, branches, hardly knowing where we were going. Where one went safely, the other followed. We often slipped and fell with a splash. When Bara sank, I pulled him up. He did the same for me. He had been right: neither of us could have gone unless there were two.

I cannot tell you how long it took before we stumbled onto another island even as there was some small morning light. With a weariness that went beyond words, we crawled upon it and sat on damp earth. It was hard to know if we had traveled twenty yards or a mile.

"I don't know if I can go any more," I said.

Bara, by my side, said, "Nor I."

Feeling only half alive, we decided to stay where we were until the day was full. Our clothing, such as it was, was sodden, cold. We agreed to take turns sleeping, both of us in great need of rest. Bara put the knife down on the ground between us, so it was in reach of both.

"Touch it," he said. "So you'll know where it is."

Then, while one slept, the other kept watch over whatever might be out there.

When awake, I listened to endless sounds—chirps, barks, snaps—but never knew the cause. Though the noises told me we were hardly alone, and I knew not what made them, nothing seemed close enough to threaten. I often thought of that bit of lace and wondered if its loss was an omen. I confess, I had a deep-rooted sense that Charity was slipping away from me.

Toward full day, though it was my turn to stay awake, I fell into a deep sleep—a dangerous thing to have done. And indeed, not long after, I was pulled into a vague wakefulness by a most peculiar sensation; it was as if some heavy thing were being dragged over my chest. Thinking I was merely sensing an unhappy dream, and too sluggish to move, I opened my eyes partway. In the vague light I saw a large black snake moving over me.

In an instant, I was fully awake, but somehow had the wits—or more likely just gripped by terrifying fear—so I dared not move, though my heart was hammering harder than it had ever done.

The snake paused, lifted its large head, and opened its fanged mouth and hissed, so I could see whiteness therein. It was a cottonmouth. Poisonous.

As I lay there it slithered on, moving off me and toward Bara.

As slowly and silently as I dared, I reached to where I recalled the knife lay and let my hand settle round the handle. When I was sure I held it tightly, I braced myself and in one rapid movement bolted up, and with all my strength, lunged and brought the knife, point down, on the snake. I missed its head, but pierced its tail. Just as quickly, I rolled away while yelling, "Bara!"

He woke, saw the snake, sprang up and away.

Since I had struck hard, the snake was pinned to the ground. It writhed in pain, twisting and turning like a rope trying to tie itself. Openmouthed, it spat and kept trying to strike.

Somehow Bara found a long stick and thrashed down on the beast. Under the repeated blows, the snake finally ceased moving and lay in a tangled twist of blood.

Bara and I stared at it.

"It went over me," I said, struggling for breath. "It was going toward you."

He nodded. "Guess you know now," he said, "why we needed the knife."

After making sure the snake was dead, he drew the knife free and offered the bloody thing to me. I shook my head. Though I had learned its value, I would not touch it.

I turned from the dead snake and looked about, still shivering from fright. The air was dim, gray-green, and still. I tried to make sense of where we were.

The island was two or three feet higher than the water, crowned with bushes and grasses. Here and there old twigs and branches lay about. Odd, moss-covered logs, in a state of rot, lay half submerged. A pale white flower grew among the moss. I may have seen a fish flit by, but it might just as well have been the shadow of something else. Insects hummed and invisible birds chirped. In places the murky water bubbled up for reasons I chose not to imagine. I drank the swamp water; so did Bara. There was no choice.

High above us, the upper branches of the towering trees were interwoven, while their fingerlike roots reached into the ruddy waters below. Low shrubbery and plants grew everywhere, and sharp roots poked up. Save for us, it was a world without any sign of human life. That said, I could have no doubt that animal dangers lay hidden, though at that moment, I saw no more snakes. Nor did I see people. Some—like Fitzhugh—we were trying to flee. Others, the ones called maroons, we sought. But where either was, close or far, I could not even begin to guess. Since Bara believed the maroons—and safety—were to be found deeper in, I had no choice but to believe him.

Bara must have guessed my thoughts. "We'll get there," he said.

While the incident of the snake had shaken us, no more was said. It was part of where we were. For the moment I only wanted to get away from that island.

CHAPTER FIFTY-SIX

In Which We Continue Our Flight through the Wretchedness That Was the Swamp.

Since we wished to travel west, our first task was to gain a sense of direction. It was not easy. We could only do it by the sun's placement, but with the tight mantle of cypress branches and needles above, there were only slanting bars of sunlight, so finding west took time.

At length, we came to an agreement: West was that way. Well enough, but how to move? After further study, we decided there was another island some thirty or so yards off in the direction we wished to go. In that same direction, we supposed, were the maroons. But precisely where? We had no idea.

Bara said, "Let's hope they have sentries so they'll challenge us."

I found two sticks, one longer than the other. I gave Bara the longer one and kept the shorter. "We can poke our way," I said.

I glanced back, thinking of Fitzhugh, but saw nothing to distress me. "If Fitzhugh's alive," I said, "maybe he's given up."

Bara snorted. "If he's alive, he'll come."

We eased ourselves back into the water and resumed walking. Once we reached the island we'd seen, we climbed on and rested for a brief time. The island was no different than the one we'd been on earlier, but we spotted animal footprints we hadn't seen before.

"Raccoon," said Bara. "You can eat them."

We continued, wading to the next small island, and pressed forward in that fashion all day, slow, unsteady, soaking wet, island to island, like skipping stones.

Once when I was in the lead, I would have sworn I saw eyes looking out at us. Some beast.

"Bara," I said, and pointed.

Bara, seeing it, halted. A stick lay on the surface of the water. I picked it up and threw it toward the eyes. There was a rustle of leaves, a splash, and it was gone.

"What was it?"

"No idea."

Sometimes we walked on logs. Sometimes, while wading in the water, we sank deep.

No matter how far we went, it looked the same as where we had started. What did change was my hunger, which grew as the day progressed. It had been two days since we had last eaten, in Annapolis.

At some time—I believe it was the afternoon of the second day—Bara suddenly stopped and raised his hand. His head was cocked so I knew he was listening hard.

I halted and listened, too.

Splashing noises were coming from behind us.

No need to speak. We knew its meaning. Someone was coming after us, perhaps many. There was no choice but to assume it was Fitzhugh.

Much alarmed, we looked for a place to hide. I pointed to another small island farther on. Bara moved that way.

As we advanced, I could only fret about what kind of visible trail we might be leaving and kept peering back over my shoulder. How many and who might be coming after us? Though I could see no one, I continued to hear sounds of water splashing, and now and again, shouts.

We crawled onto the island, which was covered with dense foliage. Bara pulled me up and shoved me before him, then spun around. On hands and knees he worked to smear over those muddy places that bore our footprints.

That done, we crawled dirt low through bushes and grasses, continually turning about to erase any signs of our passage. Reaching what we presumed was the island's center, we halted, lay down, and pressed ourselves into the dark, moist earth. In all this effort, we exchanged not as much as one word. We waited and listened.

What are the sounds of being chased? Voices shouting, sometimes loud, sometimes close. Now and again cries. "Here!" "There!"

But as if all the swamp creatures united with us in hiding, they ceased their random noises. The only sounds we heard were our own rapid, shallow breathing, and our pursuers.

We waited a goodly while—some hours, I think. No talking. Just painful listening, knowing only too well that if caught we would be put to death at once.

After I don't know how long, the birds, insects, and other swamp creatures resumed their buzz, chitter, and chirps. How sweet to hear. The message was clear: We were no longer being chased. The swamp that I had so much feared had become the place that protected us.

Bara and I stood up. Mud-covered from head to toe, our clothing was reduced to less than rags. No shoes. Cold. Though I could not see myself I suspected that Bara and I, equally filthy with mud, looked much the same. Misery makes people alike. We might as well have been God's first creations, pulled and newly made from the mire of this murky Eden.

"Do you think they've gone?" I asked Bara. "Are we free?"

He did not reply. Instead, he turned from me and faced the direction from which we—and the ones chasing us—had come. For a while he just stood there staring, listening with that deep stillness he sometimes had. It was even more time before he finally shifted round so I could see his face.

I can hardly describe what I saw: His face was a mix of joy and sadness both. Even as his dark eyes were bright with tears, a shy smile was on his lips, albeit given cautiously, as though not yet ready to erupt into joy.

"He's gone," he whispered, by which I knew he meant Fitzhugh. Next moment, as if suddenly building on newfound strength, he repeated the same words louder. "He's gone." Then he spread his sinewy arms wide, long fingers extended, as if to grow wings, or embrace the whole world, or draw a new universe into his heart.

For the first time since I had known him, Bara laughed. It must have come from a deeply buried place, as if stored in his heart forever and only now released. Next moment he burst into tears.

I leaped forward to give him a hug, which he returned. Thus, we clung together. In that moment, I learned a great notion: that my brother being free meant I, too, was free.

The two of us—betattered, cold, mud-laden, and hungry boys—simultaneously weeping, whooping, and laughing, performed a prancing, wild dance in a celebration of our freedom, as we laughed and cried together.

CHAPTER FIFTY-SEVEN

In Which, Within the Swamp, We Make a Huge Discovery.

For the rest of that long day we continued to wade through the swamp until darkness kept us from seeing what lay ahead. As was now our way, we took refuge on another island. Near ravenous, we found some berries and here and there mushrooms to nibble, and could only hope they'd do us no harm. We also drank more ruddy water. Thankfully finding the island a somewhat dryer place than the one before, we settled among the greenery as much as we could for the night. While it might seem strange to say, we had a great need to dry our feet after walking through mud and water for three days.

"Do you think we've truly gotten away?" I asked Bara.

"Think so," he said.

"But—are we lost?"

"If I'm free," he said, "how can I be lost?" But the joy I had heard before was dimmed.

I wished to think us free, and kept reminding myself that we had successfully escaped, Bara from slavery, I from convict bondage. Surely, we must soon reach the maroons—if they were truly here. Let it be admitted, I had begun to doubt.

We went to sleep hungry.

In the morning, frail sunbeams woke us to greater hunger. We found more mushrooms and berries and those plants called cattails, whose roots we ate. The mushrooms were bland, the cattail roots bitter. We ate them anyway.

We caught some fish—Bara called them bullheads— by surrounding them and grabbing them with our hands in a pool of sunlight, where small fish gathered. Such was the extreme sharpness of our appetites that we tore the fish apart and ate of their sweet flesh.

We went back into the swamp, plodding on step by step, going from one little island to yet another, each one much the same as those we'd already passed. The word "endless" never seemed so real.

That said, the travel was not so hard as it was tedious. My iron collar chafed. Our feet, constantly in water, ached and grew swollen. By day we broiled; at night we were chilled. Itching insect bites covered our skin. I was grateful to have a stick to prod my way, and sometimes to support my weariness. Bara claimed the same. But mind, we barely talked.

For a good part of that day we went on and took our night's rest on yet another small island.

In the morning, the air was clotted with a thick, cool mist. It billowed up from the swamp waters, as if a cloud had descended from the sky, making the world that much more obscure. When Bara woke and looked about, he announced, "I have no idea where we are."

"None?"

"None."

"How far do you think we've come?"

"Miles, hopefully."

"Any idea how we could find those people?"

"The whole thing is," he said, "they don't want to be found. That's the reason they hide. If they were easy to find, they wouldn't be there."

"Where's there?"

Bara waved a hand, which seemed to suggest anywhere and nowhere all at once. The gray-green mist rolled around us.

"Could we have passed them?"

"Possible."

"Maybe," I offered, "they'll find us."

"I pray." He did not sound encouraged.

We climbed off the island, got back into the water, and

continued going in what we believed was the right direction. The miasma meant we could not see far.

We waded on all that day, island to island. The green mist remained thick. The world had become simultaneously small, yet endless.

It had turned to twilight, and I was in the lead, both of us exhausted after a day of trudging, when I heard a severe *crack*. The sound came so abruptly and sharply, and different enough to what we'd become accustomed, it made us halt at once.

Bara came up close. "Where?" he whispered.

"There." I pointed to the island toward which we were aiming. We could barely see it.

"Don't move," said Bara.

We remained still, gazing into the billowing mist.

Moments later we heard a splash.

We stared in the direction from which we thought the sound had come. Then, as if it were being fashioned whole from the vaporous green and shadowy air, something vaguely human emerged. It was moving in our direction and in shape appeared large, with a head and long arms.

Bara, who had the knife, lifted it.

I was not raised to be superstitious, to be a believer in demons, witches, or hellish spirits. Yet, to see the form of a man—if that is what it was—in all that dull green obscurity, to hear the steady plash of water as he strode deliberately through the swamp toward us, was not just alarming, but so disquieting that we could only stand and gawk.

As he drew closer, I saw that the creature was bulky, crouched over, with massive arms and a fierce, dark face. In one hand—if it was a hand—was a stick, a musket, a spear—I could not tell.

We began to back up.

As the creature advanced slowly, he must have reached a point where he could see us clearly for the first time, because, even as we began to retreat, he halted and then leaned forward, as if he was as uncertain of us as we were of him.

In the gloom, then, the three of us—this swamp man, for so I considered him, Bara, and I—gazed at one another as if mutually disbelieving.

"Are you . . . *boys?*" the man suddenly cried out in a deep voice. It was as if he doubted *his* senses.

"We are," returned Bara. "Are you a man?"

"I am."

It was I who said, "Please you, sir, are you . . . dead . . . or alive?"

CHAPTER FIFTY-EIGHT

The Swamp Man.

Who are you?" replied the man. "Why are you here?" He had halted knee-deep in the water, as if uncertain about coming closer or what to do with us.

"We're trying to get free," said Bara. "Do you mean to do us any harm?"

The man pointed to Bara. "Are you a slave? And you"—he pointed at me—"you've got a convict collar."

"We're runaways," I called.

"Both?" The man continued to hold his stick as if to strike.

"Both," returned Bara. He pointed to himself. "Slave." He pointed to me. "Transported convict."

"How far have you come?"

"Miles. From the bay," I said.

"Where are you heading?"

I looked to Bara that he might answer.

"To the free people. Maroons."

"How do you know about them?"

"Talk in Annapolis," Bara replied, and quickly gave such particulars that he could.

At Bara's words, the man lowered his stick and actually offered up a smile. "Then you've done well," he said. "I'm one of the free people. I keep watch. I can take you there."

To say we felt release is the least of it. We had finally arrived where we wanted to be, as if the way to Heaven had been revealed.

The man said, "My name is Ellick. What are your names?"

"Bara."

"Oliver."

"Are there any more with you?"

"Just us."

"You can follow me," said the man. He spoke with slow clarity, while his gaze shifted back and forth between Bara and me, as if to make sure we both understood him.

He turned and we went along. As we moved I saw Ellick fully. He was a large, powerful man. His body—he wore no shirt—was muscular. He was wearing some kind of cloth trousers. As for his face, such as I could see, it was broad, with a large nose and a big mouth, his eyes capped by bushy eyebrows. He also had a dark, full beard. I hardly had to wonder why such a man might be a sentry. He would be hard to get around.

As we climbed on the island where he had been on watch, he held out a large hand to us. "You are welcome," he said, first to Bara and then to me. Powerful though he was, there was an ease about him, as if he was confident of his strength.

He led us to a cleared space from where he must have been watching. "Sit," he said. "I need to hear your stories."

Bara quickly told Ellick who he was and where he had come from. Then I told my tale. He made no comment on what we said, though now and again he nodded as if to say, "I know of that."

"Fine," said Ellick when we had finished, "I'll lead you to our settlement."

"Is it far?" I asked.

"No," was all he would say.

Bara and I exchanged looks of relief, and I tell you true, the looks were more grins than anything else.

CHAPTER FIFTY-NINE

The Secret People.

J ust how Ellick made his way through the thick swamp, I could not determine, but lead us he did. Nor can I accurately explain the path we followed. What's more, even if I could, I would not. The maroon community lay hidden in the swamp, its existence needing to remain secret. If discovered by Fitzhugh and his like, it would have been destroyed and the people who lived there slaughtered— like Clark had been—or returned to slavery.

Eventually we arrived at another island, bigger than most we had seen. As with other swamp isles, its topmost ground was a few feet higher than the water level and hidden by thick foliage and trees. Completely concealed among the greenery and cypress trunks were some five huts—as I believe they were called.

They stood on posts that lifted them higher than the land—protection against rising waters—and were built of cypress staves held together, as far as I could see, by vines and mud. A ladder stood before each entryway. Layers of swamp grass lay upon the roofs. I saw one log canoe.

Each hut provided shelter for two or three adults. Thus, in this community, some fourteen adults—men and women both—and two children made up the entire group. Most were former black slaves. Two had been indentured whites. All were runaways and had lived together some while, one or two for a number of years. Others had come recently, but I did not seek to learn the particulars. If I had asked, I don't believe I'd have been informed.

We were welcomed, given food and drink, and asked to tell our story. There was much concern about who had chased us—when, where, how many—which we answered as best we could. Then we were given a place to sleep, on grass mats under one of the huts.

That night Bara and I slept—oh rarity!—with perfect calm.

In the morning, I learned more about these people. They lived as one large clan. They worked and gathered food together, supported one another. They struggled with the swamp, struggled for food—which was not abundant—sometimes argued or disputed, but overall existed in harmony. They were a serious people but could laugh. The two children ran about—as much as they could. Everyone looked after them.

There was one elderly, white-haired woman, her face quite wrinkled, to whom all paid much respect. In the time that I was there, perhaps a month, when important decisions were made—to build another hut, to talk to another maroon community once about whether a marriage should take place—they gathered together and always requested of this woman what she thought.

For the most part these people spent their time surviving: taking care of the children, repairing huts (which were flimsy and easily damaged), hunting and fishing, growing enough food to sustain themselves. Their clothing was a mix of old cloth and animal skins. They had no firearms, but had fashioned wooden spears, fishing hooks made from a few bent nails, and one bow (that I saw) with a few arrows. One person had a knife. Bara gave Fitzhugh's knife to someone, so they had two. Over time I saw a hammer, a small scythe, and an iron pincer, or what was called pliers. Also, an iron pot. How they got them I have no idea.

Two days after we arrived, Ellick came to me. "Oliver, do you wish us to take off your collar?" More than willing, I went with him. First, he used that small iron pincer, and after twisting the nail that kept my collar together, removed it. Then he and another man, whose name was

Joshua, bade me stand still. Each gripped the iron band with their two hands. Though I felt some pain, they wrenched the collar open and were able to pull the hateful thing away. Once off they dangled the iron collar before me, and I was able to rejoice, free of that ghastly weight, emblem of my harsh condition.

But note: The iron was not thrown away. Nor was that nail. Metal was too rare a thing for them to waste. To what use they were put I don't know, but these people kept to the maxim "Good or bad, all things have purpose."

While we were there one of the men, named Joseph, left for a few days. When he returned he brought five iron nails. Since they were used as spear points and for fishing, they were deemed a great treasure.

As for meat, the people fished and hunted small creatures such as raccoon and squirrel. They made do with traps and wooden spears. They dried the meat in the open air. Skins were used for many things, from shoes to bags to haul water.

On nearby islands they grew patches of corn, sweet potatoes, and squash. The husks of dried squash were cut into spoons and other utensils. Cooking was done in small fire pits, so smoke would be slight and not give them away. The food was often wrapped in leaves and baked in hot ash, and indeed they called what they made ash cakes. It was good.

We learned there were several such small communities nearby in the swamp area—at most a mile apart but all distinct from one another. They stayed small for safety's sake, but could join together in defense of their existence when or if necessary. They had that canoe, by which they could, and did, visit one another.

Their major task was to protect themselves from the villains of the outside world. No matter how long they were free, there was always the danger of recapture by slaveholders. Much time then was spent on watch, as Ellick had been, so as not to be discovered. I think they always were on guard and prepared for flight, assuming they were being forever hunted.

In the time I was with them, Bara and I were required to be part of all. Thus I learned to harvest food from the swamp from plants that grew there, to hunt creatures that lived about. To fish.

Bara and I were taken to a little island where corn was grown. We were set to weed, which was hard, but as we worked I thought how different it was to tend the land for your people and not a master.

I learned more of field work in the time I was among those people than in all my time with Fitzhugh. I cannot know if I changed, but surely Bara did. The silence that was so much of him melted away. He talked readily to these people and did so constantly, as if he had stored up his words for a long time and only now found full release. He talked more to me, too, and everything he said was painted with eager thoughts and ideas, what he might do and become. He was simmering with excitement, happy to be himself as never before. It was indeed as if he had grown wings.

While no one told Bara and me that we had to leave the community, in our private talk we felt obliged to do so. It was but a tiny group, and though we worked alongside them, more than once we had been asked if we had plans. We were told that there were other communities—farther west—that needed people. The meaning was clear. For safety's sake, it could only be so big. At some point, we must go. Nonetheless, Bara and I took great pleasure in living there, and for that short while, chose not to do anything but live.

I did ask if anyone knew about Philadelphia. One man did—his name was Ned. He confirmed what Mr. Lunbog said, that it was north and best reached by water.

I told Bara.

"We should stay together," he said. "Go farther west. One of their other places. Ellick told me there were Indians who would welcome us. He also said that in the south the Spanish would welcome us."

I could not, would not say anything against that except, "I promised I would find my sister."

Bara remained silent for some time, staring out into the swamp. At length he turned to me. "Then we'll have to go different ways," he said. "I won't be a slave again."

I said, "You saved me."

"And you saved me," he returned.

But by unspoken consent, we did not talk further about this matter. We just knew a parting would soon come.

And sure enough, early one morning there came a cry: "They're coming. They're coming."

CHAPTER SIXTY

In Which My Life Turns a Different Way.

I n an instant, all became commotion. We hardly understood what was happening, but learned soon enough. A watchman had detected a party of white men—armed with muskets—working through the swamp. Whether they were looking for this particular community or Bara and me hardly mattered. The people had to flee deeper into the swamp, moving farther west.

They were dashing about, gathering what things they could. The old woman was led into the dugout canoe, the two children with her, fore and aft. Two other women got into the water, and with one on either side, guided the craft away.

It was astonishing to me how quickly the maroons fled. Within moments, Bara and I were the only ones on the island. We stood on its edge watching the last of the island people moving through the swamp, becoming invisible.

"I'm going with them," Bara announced. "You should come with me."

I made no answer but looked toward the east. I could not see anyone coming, but I had no doubt hunters were there, moving toward us.

Bara stepped into the water. "Oliver, we need to go now. If we lose them we may not find them again."

I said, "I'm going to Philadelphia."

"Then you'll have to go alone. I won't go back."

"I know."

"What if you can't find Charity?"

"Bara, I have to try."

He stared at me for a moment then went farther into the water.

Remaining where I was, I hardly knew what to say. How was I to say good-bye to the one who had saved my life so many times, in so many ways? How to say good-bye to him I admired above all, who I wished I might become? All well to say I must find my sister. Bara had become my brother. In Bara I had never known a braver, smarter person. I am not ashamed to say I had tears in my eyes. I could see it was the same for him.

"I think you'll find her," he said.

"Do you really believe it?"

He smiled. "You've become bigger, smarter."

I said, "Who will you find?"

"I've already found my people."

We gave each other an embrace. Then he stepped farther away into the swamp waters.

"Bara," I called.

He looked back.

"Do you think," I cried, "we'll ever see each other again?"

"In this world, the only way they'll let us be together is in our thoughts. Seek me there. I'll seek you."

Then he moved off, wading through the swamp in the direction the others had gone.

I wanted to shout after him. But—thinking of those who were coming—I felt constrained to whisper, "Stay free."

He did not look back again. I chose to think he could not.

I waited until I could see him no more, until he was gathered into the swamp. As I stood there my heart misgave me. You cannot do this alone, I told myself. Go with him.

I suspect if I had seen my friend one more time, if he had turned, I think I would have followed. But when

I looked west, Bara was no longer in sight. Perhaps it was my tears that blinded my eyes.

I turned to face east. Can I do it? I asked myself.

The only answer I received was: You either do or die.

CHAPTER SIXTY-ONE

In Which I, Quite Alone, Travel into the Swamp.

Let it be understood: I didn't know who was coming. Was it Fitzhugh? Even if Fitzhugh was not among them, I assumed there were many, and well armed. Yet, I could neither hear nor see anything of them. It was as if I was being chased by unseeable men.

Feeling urgency I stepped into the swamp and moved as fast as I could from the maroon island, hoping I would not be heard. I reached one island. A second. A third. I climbed the fourth and all but buried myself in its leafy center. Then all I could do was wait, listen, and hope. I had two great fears: what these people might do to me, and what they might force me to say about the maroons. If they caught the smallest sight of me, all would be lost.

At one point, I heard voices from a distance. Not anyone in particular. What I heard loudest was my beating heart. Happily, I never heard gunshots, which suggested the maroons were free. But that, too, I would never truly learn. Then, after a goodly time, I heard no more threatening sounds. I told myself it was safe.

All the same, I kept thinking about Bara. Had I done the right thing to separate from him? To contain myself and keep still, I tried to think about Charity, how I might reach her.

All very well to say I would find her in Philadelphia. My sole sense of the proper path was what the maroon and Mr. Lunbog told me: that the city was north and east from Annapolis. Clearly, I must travel that way.

The direction from which Bara and I had fled from Fitzhugh held, for an absolute certainty, the greatest danger. But I had been informed that the best way to reach Philadelphia was by water. One hundred and twenty miles north, said Mr. Lunbog. The great bay ran north, the very direction I needed to go. Surely it would be far easier to paddle up the bay than to walk. There was a canoe at Fitzhugh's plantation. I might use it but I knew to get to it would take days of sodden marching.

Foolhardy, perhaps, to return to Fitzhugh's place to secure that canoe, but had not my life worked that way so far? It could not be all folly. Surely, at some point, risk might become reward. Besides, I had absolutely no knowledge of where else I might find another boat.

When Bara looked for the maroon community, he said we must go straight west. Well then, I must go straight east. Pleased to have a strategy, however hazardous, I paused long enough to find a stout stick to help me walk. If I waited any longer, I would lose whatever courage—you may just as well call it folly—I had.

I stepped into the swamp, using my stick as prod, and set off. Going from island to island, I moved opposite from the way Bara and I had come.

The water, to be sure, was not solid, but nonetheless required effort to push through. Many a time I slipped and dropped down, floundering up to my neck. At such moments, panic would seize me, and the stick became my vital if humble rescuer. Oh, how I missed Bara. But rather than dwell on that, I kept telling myself, I must do this.

When I reached islands, I climbed on and made myself rest. In spite of my hunger I paused only long enough to determine my position and gather my strength. Then I selected my next goal—another island—and waded on, yet again, as if I were a skipping stone.

I shall not bore you with the small particulars of my journey, because it was much the same no matter how far I went. Of course, I grew exhausted. At such times, I would find an island, get on it, reach its middle place, and sleep, albeit restlessly. Food—scant, to be sure—was where I found it: cattails, and twice a fish. I did not travel at night.

After three days, I was cold, numb, and beyond tired. Still, I sensed I was approaching my goal. I therefore forced myself on until I recognized the area. Then I was sure I had come close to Fitzhugh's land. That meant, of course, I had come to the hardest part of my journey: to get hold of the canoe.

You must believe me but it was only then did I remember that whereas the canoe was presumably by Fitzhugh's wharf, the paddle was in the chest inside his house. I had no doubt I would be able to get the canoe, but it would be useless without the paddle.

That would require me to go inside Fitzhugh's house. Need I say it: my fear was that he would be there.

CHAPTER SIXTY-TWO

My Return to Fitzhugh's House and What I Discovered.

I retreated to the nearest island and worked to gather up my courage. It was dark when I finally waded out of the swamp and ventured onto firm ground, which I knew as Fitzhugh's plantation. In so doing I was reminded how I came off the *Owners Goodwill* onto land.

I was wet from my waist down, hungry with an uneasy pain in my chest. All that said, uppermost in my thoughts was this: Would the old man be here?

I moved with caution through the dark woods, watching and listening for any hint that would tell me if Fitzhugh or anyone else was about. I did hear noises: snaps, rustling of leaves, quick cracklings, which always caused me to halt. But I neither saw nor heard anything to alarm me, or so I told myself. Even so, I had to force myself to move forward. Thus, I pressed forward, my eyes constantly shifting over the landscape, ever ready to flee.

It wasn't long before I crept out from beneath the protection of the trees. The moon and trembling stars hung in a cloudless sky, providing just enough light that I could see. That meant, as I was all too aware, I was likewise visible. The air was cool enough to make me shiver, but I suspect it was caused by great unease.

I pressed on slowly—my body half-stooped—until I came upon a field of tobacco, which I recognized as the farthest from the old man's house. The large leaves were brown. When a finger of breeze stirred them, they crinkled like old parchment paper, the sound grating on my nerves.

I halted and surveyed the field. Weeds were abundant. The tobacco had not been tended.

When I reached the next field, or what should have been the field, it was not there. It was a sullied patch of land, a black scar burned to nothing.

I stood still. From my vantage point I could see the entire plantation. As for Fitzhugh, I saw no sign, but reminded myself how devious he was.

I moved on and saw another field of standing tobacco. Then another that was burned. The pigsty was empty, which I took as another good sign.

I continued on toward Fitzhugh's house but went past it to the stable. There was no horse. That eased me more.

Do not be fooled by good signs, I told myself. I think the words came in Bara's voice.

I stepped around to the front of the house and studied it from a safe distance. Under the moonlight, it appeared as before, in a state of shabbiness, no worse or better than it had been. I studied it. Most unusual: The door stood open. No light came from within. Though nothing suggested Fitzhugh was about, I reminded myself that if he was there, he would be sleeping—and his pistol would be by his side.

Did I really need to go in? I asked myself and just as quickly gave myself the answer: I had to get the paddle.

I approached the door and listened, as before, intently. I heard nothing. I finally put my hand to the door and gave it a small shove, so that it groaned. The familiar sound made my stomach squeeze.

I waited. Nothing happened. The smell of rum floated out. That stopped me too. But the door was open enough that I could stick my head through and look about.

It was darker inside, of course, but my first observation suggested it was deserted.

Emboldened, I pushed the door farther in and stood upon the threshold. I could see no evidence that anyone was there. As my eyes adjusted to the darkness inside, I saw that the furniture, such as it was, was tumbled. The musket that always hung on the far wall was gone. The chest lid stood open. Some withered apples lay about. Cold ashes were on the floor. The bed was turned over and empty. The place had been ransacked.

Bolstered—but with my heart thudding in my ears—I went to his chest and looked within. To my great relief the paddle was still there. I gathered it up. When I saw the fishing spear I took that, too, elated to have it.

With a feeling of great release, I moved out of the house and set off at a half run—paddle and spear in hand—toward the bay and the wharf. I was halfway down the slope when I came upon a mound of earth. Though the light was gloomy I could see the ground had been newly dug. Though it looked like the approximate shape of a grave—I was reminded of Clark's grave—there was no marker. But on top of the mound was Fitzhugh's battered hat.

Did he lie buried there? I did not know, but I suspected as much.

It held me for a moment. Had he died in the fire? Or was it his fury that killed him after Bara and I had run? Let me confess, no feeling of reverence or forgiveness came from me. No joy either. But I did something I had never done, and hoped to never do again: I spat upon that grave. I wanted to believe he was gone, and was being given his deserved punishments elsewhere. I pondered what would be the worst retribution: I decided upon an eternity alone, in the company of himself.

I hurried on.

I reached the wharf. The canoe was there. It took some struggle and strength—but I had gained in that, and managed to pull it free. I set it into the bay water. I placed the paddle and the spear within. Finally, I crawled in myself.

Trying to remember what Bara had taught me—wishing with yet another painful surge of emotion that he was with me—I paddled out into the bay. Its waters were dark but calm. Once offshore, I turned my little ship in what I believed was the direction that would lead me to Philadelphia, Black Horse Alley, the bakery of Master Isaac Bell, and Charity.

CHAPTER SIXTY-THREE

My Voyage up the Chesapeake Bay.

At first, my lack of skill, plus my eagerness to get away, caused the heavy canoe to meander and sway precariously so that more than once I was sure I must capsize. I took some moments to remind myself of what I had done, that I could take care of myself, that I had learned many skills. I can do this, I kept telling myself. I am not the boy who was in Melcombe Regis. I further told myself that I needed to be calm and resolute and kept on making advancement in my paddling skills with every stroke.

Happily, the bay, though vast, was unruffled, and the moon provided all the light I needed to be rewarded by progress.

I did allow myself to think how astonishing that I was where I was. Not long ago, what I was doing, being in America, in a canoe, upon the vast Chesapeake, perfectly alone, would have been utterly impossible to imagine. Life, it is commonly said, is full of possibilities. Let it also be acknowledged: Life is also full of impossibilities. Who is to say which enriches one more?

As I moved up the bay I kept close to the shore. Now and again I saw a wharf much like the one owned by Fitzhugh. I saw buildings, too, dark in the night. There were small islands, but whether occupied or not I did not know.

I paddled until I was too tired to paddle more. Then I edged into an empty shore, a place where forest reached the bay. I pulled the bow of the canoe on land, lay down within it, and instantly slept.

I woke to a different kind of day. The sky was gray. The waters of the bay were unsettled with a wind blowing hard from the north. Feeling I had gained enough skill to continue, I pushed the canoe into the water, climbed in, and began to paddle. With an eye to the weather, I continued north, but made sure again to stay close to shore. The water chop and the wind made the going hard.

It was not long before the sky grew darker, and the wind increased to such violence that the bay waters tossed and turned, white and foamy. Rain began to fall in torrents. My canoe began to dip and spin, and my efforts to control it only made things worse. I decided to aim her for the shore, only to have the canoe roll when hit by a broadside wave and spill me out.

Call it fortune that let me depend on my new strength and skills. I did not lose my grip on the paddle, and that helped me remain afloat. Even so, for a moment I had no idea where I was or the location of the canoe. As I struggled and looked about the churning water, I was struck behind by the canoe. It was not so hard a blow, and my primary response was relief. I spun about and with my free hand gripped the canoe. Still holding the paddle with my other hand, I kicked my legs so that I moved toward what I could see through the rain was the shore.

In a matter of moments my feet touched bottom, which allowed me to stagger forward, the canoe still in tow. As the rain and wind lashed me, I pitched the paddle into the canoe and used both hands to reach land. Once there, I dragged the boat up, rolled it over, and crept beneath. The rain drummed over my head but I was safe.

Yes, I was cold and wet, but I was protected from the worst of the sudden weather, which did not last so long. There was something much more: I reminded myself I had survived in England, came across the ocean on a prison ship, survived convict labor, escaped from Fitzhugh, came through the swamp. I had secured

Fitzhugh's canoe and paddle and used them. I had survived yet another storm.

All of this allowed me to remind myself yet again I was not what I had once been. I no longer felt as if I was a boy. I was in command of my free life. There would be—I promised myself—no more unexpected turns.

CHAPTER SIXTY-FOUR

Ever Closer to Philadelphia.

In the morning, I came out from beneath the canoe to look up to a gray but rainless sky. The squalls had passed on. I was alive; I had the canoe and the paddle. All I had lost was the fishing spear when the canoe capsized.

Though still fearful of discovery, I set out with the canoe upon the bay once again. Before long I perceived one of those small islands and aimed for the smallest, since I could see that there were no people on it.

I came ashore, pulled the canoe up high among some bushes, and hid it. It was then I allowed myself to feel my full exhaustion. Without much thought, I lay down on the ground and slept.

I think I slept for most of the day. When I woke, it was with great hunger. I searched about and found some of the plants that Bara had taught me I might eat. Then

I recalled his oysters. I waded into the water, got on my hands and knees, and searched on the sandy bottom. It was less a case of my finding them, as they found me when I felt a sharp pain.

Gingerly I rooted about, found the object I wanted, and pulled up an oyster some seven inches long. I searched again with greater care and found three more. Then—again as Bara had done—I banged them together, shattering the shells. This time I ate without revulsion, indeed with elation befitting my deep hunger.

Bara, I thought, once again, you have taught me how to save myself.

I made myself stay on that island for a whole day, so as to regain my strength and gain a sense of security.

The next morning, much refreshed, I returned the canoe to the water and with some six oysters in the bow I continued my voyage north.

In the days to come as I paddled, I did see people, but none seemed to take much notice of me, a person in a canoe going slowly northward upon the vast bay. Was I not the perfect image of this brand-new world?

I went by many islands, small and large. I saw porpoises. In the sky, birds were plentiful. Now and again I saw fish, either in the water or leaping. Many a time I wished I had the spear.

On those broad waters were also sailing ships of

different sizes, some quite big, others small. I must have been observed but no one hailed me or required me to come ashore. Did they consider me with a spyglass? I had no idea.

Since I no longer wore my iron collar, I told myself I would not be apprehended as an escaped convict. Nonetheless, I took the precaution to invent a story I could tell if I were stopped and questioned. I decided to say that my (invented) master—a Mr. Trigg—had gone to Philadelphia, and being his servant, I was belatedly required to join him.

I pushed on, one day after another. Surely, my skills increased since there is no better teacher than a desire to arrive somewhere. By way of a bonus, I observed magnificent dawns of deep pinks as well as splendid sunsets of reds, purples, and oranges. When nights advanced, I searched for small islands, and after making sure—as best I could—that they were uninhabited, took myself on land. Dawn had me moving again.

For six days, I journeyed north. It was only after all that time that I began to notice that the bay was narrowing. I continued to maneuver my way in a northeast direction—the way I wanted to go—until I found myself in what I supposed was a river. By that time, I was no longer fearful of people, and once, twice, I pulled to shore and spoke to those laboring in the fields.

"Can you tell me how I can reach Philadelphia?" I would ask.

They would point, tell me how far, seventy miles, fifty, thirty, and I would paddle on.

At length, the river I was on—the Elk River, I had learned—became too small for me to paddle my canoe any farther. At that place, I simply abandoned the little craft and left it for others. Then I proceeded northward along roads that seemed well used. Since I continually asked my way, I encountered many farms and some people. How I must have appeared to them, in tatters, filthy, I could hardly imagine.

What I gained by it all was an understanding that I was truly approaching my goal: Philadelphia. By then I had also learned to give a better explanation for my isolated travel. Now my story was that I had been shipwrecked somewhere near Annapolis, and thereby separated from my Philadelphia family, and was trying to reach my true home. That allowed me to account for my tattered clothing. Of course, I was not being honest in giving such an account, but I assuaged my discomfort by telling myself that it was not entirely untrue. To say I had been shipwrecked—considered as a metaphor—had much reality to it.

"How come thou here?" I was asked more than once.

I would tell my shipwreck story, and must have done

it well, for I was treated well. I thus learned that nothing encourages an inventor of tales to embellish more than food and kindness.

Thus, I made my way to the shores of the wide Delaware River until, as I continued to walk my way north by that great flow, I beheld, albeit at a distance, the city of Philadelphia. Just to see it filled me with a sense of excitement.

Charity was there.

I could have no doubt: my journey was almost at an end.

CHAPTER SIXTY-FIVE

In Which I Finally Come to Philadelphia Only to Experience Yet Another Unexpected Change.

It was in the late autumn of 1725—almost a full year after all these events began, which I have chosen to call my unexpected life—when I reached Philadelphia, the second largest city (London being the first) in the entire British world. I reached it at night, but I continued to trudge along, utterly determined to find my sister that same eve, knowing that to see her face would fill the sky with brightness. I could hardly keep from running.

Guided by such lights as there were, I walked along Water Street by the Delaware River, and thereby entered the big city. I considered pausing and waiting till the morning. I was far too impatient. I was all but there!

Though Philadelphia was not fifty years old, it had a

population of some eleven thousand. I found it laid out in perfect squares, and while the streets were unpaved, they were lined with rows of small, plain houses mostly built of brick. It was far advanced over Annapolis, and much more orderly than London. The Delaware River bankside was thick with wharfs and many ships. Indeed, what I immediately saw, though it was night, was that Philadelphia was a crowded, prosperous city with a sense of purpose.

Only a few people were upon the streets. Wishing to know where Black Horse Alley was, I approached one, then two people, only to have them look at me and no doubt appraise me as without merit for they pointedly told me to keep my distance.

Only then did I fully acknowledge how shameful I must have looked in rags, bare feet, hair longish, filthy with dust and grime. The murk of night could only have added to my frightfulness. It made me that much more eager to find Master Isaac Bell's bakery and my sister.

My assumption was that Charity had found employment there, and as was often the case, lived with her master and perhaps mistress. I would throw myself upon the baker's mercy and plead for an audience with Charity. Never mind the hour. I could not wait.

As I was wandering about in a blind search for Black Horse Alley, I observed two men on the street walking side by side, each with a lantern in hand. Burly fellows, they seemed sober men going about some business. One of them also had a cudgel.

I approached them. "Sirs," I called. "A little service."

They halted, lifted their lamps, and considered me gravely.

Before I could say one word more, one of them said, "Who art thou?"

"And it please you, sirs, my name is Oliver. I was shipwrecked somewhere near Annapolis and separated from my family, and am trying to reach my true home, which is here in Philadelphia."

"And where is thy home?"

"Black Horse Alley."

"Dost thou live there?"

"Since I was born, sirs."

"Then how can thee *not* know where it is?"

"It's . . . it's dark, sir. And I'm . . . very tired."

"Have thee run away from home?" one of them said, to which the other added, "Or your apprenticeship?"

"No, sir, I . . ."

"There is a law against vagrancy," said the first. "And we are the night watch."

Their hostile tone shook me. I was so near to all my purpose, my final goal, the finding of Charity, only to be rudely blocked.

On the instant, I realized I had blundered. I had lied.

Gone to the wrong people. The folly of what I had done—for I had brought this on myself—was as if I had picked up a stone, swallowed it, only to have it lodged in my throat. It was unbearable. Infuriating to the extreme. I could not bear it.

I started to run—not that I knew where to go. I took the first turning to find that I had plunged into a blocked passageway. I spun about, only to have the two night watchmen come down upon me. In a desperate fury, I pitched myself at them, in hopes of breaking through. My reward was a great clout on the head. It was a dark night, but things went darker still.

When I regained my senses, I found myself being bodily hauled along the city streets by the two men. Mortified and infuriated at being apprehended yet again, I could barely breathe. How true the old adage: "A race is not fully run till you cross the final line." Never mind that I had seen that line. The painful truth was that I had not reached it. The even more painful truth was that it was my own impatience that had done me over. What had Bara urged upon me? Patience. But patience goes for naught if, at the very last, the smallest moment, you toss that patience away. Patience is naught if it is not all the time.

"Where are you taking me?" I managed to ask.

"Jail."

The Philadelphia jail was a stone building on the

corner of Third and High Streets, in the middle of the city.

Straightaway, I was thrown into a gloomy hole. The brief light that accompanied my entry—before the door was shut tight behind me and loudly locked—revealed a number of people on the floor, asleep.

My head in pain, my heart equally so, I looked about and found a vacant bit of hard wall. There I slumped down to the equally hard floor, and in profound despondency, gave myself over to silent, chest-aching sobs. Oh, to have come to this. Never has close seemed so far.

That said, I was so worn out, in heart and soul, I soon cried myself asleep. My last thought that day was: What can possibly happen to me now?

CHAPTER SIXTY-SIX

In Which I Am Required to Go Before Another Judge and What Happened.

I woke next morning to find myself among a rag-tag group of men and women, who were, or so they informed me, mostly debtors, runaway apprentices, and various other accused persons waiting to be tried. They paid no particular attention to me, so that I am not sure they knew—or cared—that I was among them. The talk amongst themselves was full of angry prattle about the unfairness of life and law, their own absolute innocence, and their sure knowledge about the new judge who was presiding over the court.

In that regard, some conveyed, with much evidence, his savage contempt for people and their crimes. He was, they said, "a hanging judge." Yet others insisted he was a most kindly man, and would surely let everyone go free. Another claimed this judge had recently come from England and brought along all the cruelty of that nation's laws. All of which to say, no one knew with any certainty as to what might be their fate—or mine.

If that was not worrying enough, I also learned by their talk that the local law in Philadelphia had, of late, much hardened. The pillory—into which heads, hands, and sometimes feet were locked for periods of painful time—along with a whipping post, had been newly installed. Contrary to what Mr. Lunbog had told me, the death penalty was now in full effect. I was informed that second offenders were the ones most likely to be executed. It appeared that mercy in the new world was as mute as it was in the old.

It took little imagination for me to predict the offences of which I would be found guilty. I was an unattached boy, a vagrant without money, friends, or home. Yes, I was, or so presumed, close to Charity. That only served to increase my agony. Hardly to be wondered that my mind was in such a state that I wished to have my life come to a speedy end one way or another.

As I waited, however, I concocted a plan: I would go before the judge and beg that my sister be sent for. Surely, she would protect me. Assert my character. Plead for me.

It was perhaps mid-morning when the turnkey arrived. With apparent randomness, he selected a few to go before the judge.

That is when I stood up. "Please, sir," I called out. "Take me."

The turnkey considered me curiously. "Why should I?" he demanded.

"I wish to come to the end of all this."

"To hang?"

"If I must."

The other prisoners looked upon me as if I were mad. No doubt, I was.

"If that's what you want, come along. You'll find our new judge happy to fulfill your request."

He led the group of us out of the jail to the court building nearby. Unlike in England, we were not chained together, but we few prisoners were tightly walked by bailiffs and their size and whips were sufficient to overawe us. Not that I needed coaxing. I wished everything done, done. I would have run to trial.

As for the courthouse, compared to the other structures I had seen in that city, it was much finer. Made of brick, it was of two levels, with a large door facing out to a grand balcony on the second level.

Beneath that elegant balcony were a pillory and a whipping post. Realizing my plan to summon Charity was only my latest folly, and presuming I would receive a sentence of execution, I gazed mournfully upon these instruments of punishment.

Matching flights of stairs led up to the balcony and the wide entry door. Flanking the door were large windows with diamond-shaped glass panes, which curiously reminded me of the windows at the Swan Inn, the place that Mr. Sandys's mother kept—and where I met Captain Hawkes. That my life was repeating itself made me ever more willing to embrace the extreme judgment sure to come. The law had not served me well. Like an octopus, it had many arms to clutch at me. I could not escape.

We went through the balcony door and into the court. You may recall that the court in London where I received my sentence of transportation was in the open air. This court was different. To begin, it was inside. At the far end of the room was a high and empty desk, where I presumed the judge presided. To the right was a jury box of two levels. A table and chairs stood before the judge's place. There was also a large cage, which, as I was about to learn, was where the prisoner stood.

There were also benches for observers to sit. A few were present, a rather motley crew, there, I supposed, to enjoy the legal theater.

When I entered, a jury was already sitting in the box. These men were bewigged, all of them looking fairly prosperous by way of garb.

At the table were other men, equally well dressed.

You may be sure I was well aware that I was not only

in rags, but filthy. I probably stank. There are some who claim that Justice is blind, but I never heard of any law that looked upon poverty as an advantage. Even if I could not be seen, I was sure I would be smelled out. Then too, I was thoroughly despondent, and no doubt that, too, was noticeable. There was nothing charming about me.

For whatever reason—perhaps because I appeared to be the youngest prisoner, or maybe because I had asked to be quickly judged—I was immediately sent to the accused's cage, told to stand and wait.

A gentleman entered from a side door and called out, "All rise for the honorable judge."

The people in the room did just that. The judge entered. Being in great terror, I only saw his emblems of power, the frightful blood-red robe edged with gold, his great wig, and puffy white sleeves. I had to force myself to look at the man's face and only then did I truly grasp that the judge was my father.

CHAPTER SIXTY-SEVEN

In Which My Life Has Even More
Unexpected Events.

S ince November 12, 1724, when I found myself alone in
my home in Melcombe Regis, England, midst a savage
storm, the progress of my life—if progress is the proper
word—was continually unexpected. But nothing was so
unexpected as to be reunited with my father, who had
become a judge in the court of Philadelphia.

When he recognized me—which he did with a wonder
equal to my own—he instantly recessed the court and
bade me to join him in an adjacent room. He told me to
sit before him and for some time we stared at each other,
equally mazed that we should come together in such a
place and situation.

As you may recall, my father and I were not particu-
larly emotional, one with the other. Speaking for myself I

had not been pleased with his practice of fatherhood. Nor did I think was he. As I gazed upon him, I had to wonder: Would he deny his paternity, or embrace me? All I could do was wait and learn.

He began by saying, "I know from where I came. The last time I saw you, you were on the River Thames being taken to a prison ship. How did you come here?"

"Please, sir, I came looking for my sister, Charity."

"Charity!"

"I believe she is here."

He made no comment, but gazed at me more astonished than ever. Let it be said, it is not often that a son can maze a father. I felt a kind of pride.

"Where?" he demanded.

"Here in Philadelphia. The bakery of Master Isaac Bell, Black Horse Alley."

He jumped to his feet and lifted a hand as if bestowing a blessing. "As judge of this court," he pronounced, "I herewith pardon all of your offences. Now come along."

What followed next is a scene that I would have liked to observe from a distance: a bewigged judge in his red robes, striding down Philadelphia's High Street, hand in hand with a ragged, barefoot boy. A parade of high and low.

Black Horse Alley was easily found twixt First and Second Streets, near High Street. Lo and behold—as old stories would say—the bakery was right there, a modest brick structure, with a wooden sign that bore the crude image of a loaf of bread. The door was painted green.

My father would have rushed forward but I begged him to hold back while I went. Was I not deserving of the event?

I knocked on the door. No one came. I knocked again, louder. Was there ever a longer moment?

At last the door opened.

There was my beloved Charity altogether dusted over with flour. Of course, I knew her in an instant. But she did not recognize me. "Yes?" she said. "May I help you?"

"It's me," I cried out. "Oliver."

"Oliver?" she said with some indignation. "My brother is small, fair-skinned, and clean, none of which you are."

"Charity, it's me," I cried. "And here is Father." I drew this bewigged and costumed judge, our father, in close.

For a moment, we all just looked at one another. As for who first shrieked with joy the loudest—Charity or me, or perhaps even Father—I cannot say. Suffice to say I flung my arms about my sister and thereby became equally covered by joy, tears, and flour.

Then and there, on those front bakery steps, came the endless questions asked by all of us: "Where did you come from? How did you ever come here? How did you find me?"

The simplest story came from Charity. She had been

brought to Philadelphia, but on her convict ship had been wooed by a young, free immigrant who was going to set up a bakery in Pennsylvania colony. It was mid-voyage when he actually bought her and they were married, and thus she avoided most horrors of the ocean passage.

"I don't know," she said, "if I, in the eyes of the law, am his bonded servant or his wedded wife. But he is a good man, and I love him."

Then my father related his travels:

"Surely you remember that I promised that I would follow you both to the Americas. Wishing to find you, I voyaged to Philadelphia because as I was informed, it was in the middle colonies. That seemed a place to start my search. But once I landed, my knowledge of the English law was such that once it became known, I was fairly well forced by the local government to become a judge. It seemed a new ruling party here desired to move away from what they considered the excessive softness of Quaker rule.

"Is there a better way to undermine authority," he said in his old cantankerous way, "than by joining it?"

Then it was my time.

As fast as I could, I provided them with a summary of all that had happened to me since I had last seen them in London, which you, as reader, already know.

"An astonishing story," my father said when I was done.

Then he added something the likes of which he had never said before: "I can only admire you."

To which Charity added, "Blessed be the day that we have all survived."

Thus was my family reunited in this most unexpected and delighted fashion.

I need only add we met Charity's husband, and he appeared a most decent fellow.

I do not pretend to have learned great writing skills while setting down the events of this part of my life. What I have discovered is that it is far easier to write about hardship and misery than happiness. Though contentment is the goal of most, I suspect that joyful state of being is difficult to set down in words because we do not quite know what happiness is. We merely feel it. Whereas misfortune can be measured in many words, joy is but passing brief.

Still, I can tell you true, I am wholly content, resolved that my life should have no more misery. As of this moment, I have not been drowned nor hanged. I can only hope that now that I am an American Colonial, my fate will be something else. But I am well advised that, as the saying goes, he who thinks he can foretell the future is future's fool.

I thus put down my pen, blot the pages with sand,

with the hopeful expectation that my life is done with the unexpected.

But I cannot end my story without adding this: Not a day passes when I don't think of Bara—somewhere in that swamp, or wherever he might be. Yes, I had found my sister, but I can only pray, from my deepest heart, that my brother is still free.

I remain, therefore, your most humble and faithful servant,

Oliver Cromwell Pitts

A NOTE FROM THE AUTHOR

In eighteenth-century England, London swelled in population and became more than ever a center of mass poverty and great wealth. Crime against property became commonplace. In reaction, the British government enacted harsh laws to punish both minor offenders and major criminals. This collection of laws was known as "the bloody codes." One of the results of these laws was punishment by transportation, in which those convicted of minor and serious crimes were sent to the British American colonies, where the convicts were sold for forced labor. The transportation of these convicts—men, women, and children—became a business.

Historians believe that by the time of the American Revolution, the thirteen colonies had a population of about two million, of which some fifty thousand were felons who had been sent to America from Great Britain. These felons were mostly shipped to the colonies of Maryland and Virginia to work the tobacco fields, the primary source of economic strength in America. When the mostly white felons became relatively expensive to own, more enslaved black laborers were used. There was, however, a time, as depicted in this story, when white felons and enslaved black people worked side by side.

Maroon communities were mostly made up of once-enslaved black people who escaped and lived in independent communities. These communities existed throughout North and South America. In Jamaica, there was even a long-lasting "Maroon War," in which enslaved people, joining with indigenous people, fought for their freedom.

In North America, maroon communities often lived in swamp regions. Their history is complex. But because they were by necessity secretive, knowledge of them has only recently come to light.

Felon slave labor is not widely known as part of American history. The story of the penal colony that became Australia is more familiar. But England transported felons to Australia only after the American Revolution, when the United States stopped accepting them. Perhaps the best-known novel about a transported felon is Charles Dickens's *Great Expectations*, which features a nineteenth-century convict—Magwitch—sent to Australia.